A TULLAGULLA CHRISTMAS

HEATHER REYBURN

ISBN 978-0-6451234–4-9 Print Edition

Heather Reyburn

www.heatherreyburn.com

CHAPTER 1

"Leaving?" Grace dropped the tray of scones with a clatter and gaped at her husband. "Why now? It's only three weeks until Christmas."

"Sweetheart, they deserve retirement. They've been here forever, and we both know the last couple of years have been tough. Remember—their health issues have not been trivial." Tom hugged Grace, his tall, thin frame pressing gently against her heavily pregnant stomach. Resting his chin on her head, he continued, "I know how much they'll be missed, but we can't deny them what they've earned. They'll be back to visit."

Grace sniffed. "I'm not saying they shouldn't retire. It's just that I thought they'd be with us for a bit longer —at least another year or two." She pulled away, her eyes meeting his. "They're like a second set of parents, and I'll miss everything about them, not just their friendship." The lump in her throat grew.

"We all will. Sit down, love. I'll make a cup of tea," Tom said.

Grace slumped in the chair, her mind spinning. Greg and Beth had been away from Tullagulla for nearly two weeks for medical checks and to catch up with their daughters. A wave of disappointment flooded her. She'd heard their vehicle drive past the homestead the previous night—too late for Grace to visit them. Chewing her lip, she struggled to hide her distress.

If they were going to share such important news, I would have liked to have been with Tom to hear it.

She shrugged and focused on her husband as he removed his glasses and polished them on the edge of his shirt—a reaction Grace recognised as his *gathering my thoughts* moment.

"Greg said they enjoyed their holiday at Tin Can Bay. I know it's one of their favourite places to stay—but I admit, I didn't realise that they were actually considering living there permanently."

"Did Greg tell you what their new house is like?" Grace asked.

"Not really. He said it's close to the water, so handy for him to go fishing. I'm surprised Beth hasn't been over to talk to you about it," Tom added.

Grace glanced at the kitchen clock. Ten past nine. Too early for smoko? *No, never.*

"Hellooo!" Beth's call resonated across the veranda as if on cue.

"Hi, Beth. Come and join us for a cuppa," Tom said.

He pushed the door open as the familiar figure huffed her way up the steps. Her wispy, grey hair was in even more disarray than usual, and in spite of her heavy heart, Grace melted. She moved towards her friend and hugged her, Grace's protruding belly and the older woman's stout physique preventing the physical connection they were accustomed to.

"Tom was just telling me your news," Grace said. She smiled, determined not to show Beth her wretchedness.

"Oh. I was hoping to beat him to it." Her face collapsed with disappointment, and Grace squeezed her arm.

"Don't worry. He hasn't told us much. Perhaps you could fill in the details?" Grace said.

"It all happened quite quickly really. The doctor was pleased with me—except I have to lose some weight—and Greg is okay, but he's not to work so hard. It was Hayley who suggested we buy a place and retire now while we're still active enough to make the move."

"That sounds sensible," Tom said. He poured the tea and passed the mugs to Grace and Beth.

"What made you decide on Tin Can Bay?" Grace asked.

"You know we've always liked holidaying there. Since the girls are both on the coast, it's the perfect place for us to meet. It's quiet and pretty and not too far from medical help if we need it—although I hope we've had our ration of problems." She grimaced and took a deep breath before continuing. "Hayley and

Nick live in Hervey Bay now, and with a baby on the way, we want to be close enough to help out when we can."

"And Kirstie?" Grace prompted.

"Kirstie's still busy with work and socialising but living on the north side of the city means she's not far away. She can nip up and visit us whenever she likes." Beth finished, frowning.

"Of course that's a perfect spot for you to retire. We'll miss you," Grace said, her lip quivering.

"Oh, Grace." Beth launched forwards and clasped Grace's hand.

"I'm not crying—just a bit emotional," Grace said, and shot her a watery smile.

"We're not leaving yet. We have to wait until the house up there is vacant anyway, so we'll have Christmas here and organise our move sometime in January."

"So, you'll still be with us for the baby?" Grace asked.

"Of course. And hopefully the wedding—that is, if Bronte and Cameron don't muck about too long. I told Greg I'm not leaving Tullagulla until after the little one makes an appearance and I get to meet him or her," Beth finished firmly. She pulled a handkerchief out of her apron pocket and dabbed her face. "I won't be sorry to get away from this heat though and feel the sea breeze again."

Tears threatened and Grace gulped as a wave of

self-pity washed over her. She blinked them away and swallowed a mouthful of tea.

"I'm sorry I've upset you, Grace. You know I don't mean to," Beth said softly.

"I'm just being silly. I don't know why my emotions are all over the place at the moment."

"I know why. You're in the final weeks of your pregnancy, it's stinking hot, and everyone's stressed about the drought. Now Greg and I have announced that we're going to up and leave you after living here for thirty-six years—just to top it all off. I reckon your emotions are perfectly normal given the circumstances."

Grace smiled at Beth's matter-of-fact explanation. She prided herself on being sensible and strong. Maybe Beth was right—it was just hormones.

"Your friendship and support when I first arrived on Tullagulla was unbelievable. You've been a nanny to Daniel, a second mother to me, and confidante when the going got tough." Grace paused. "I'll miss you."

Beth shoved her chair back and got to her feet before reaching out and hugging Grace again. "Don't be silly. We've been lucky to have each other—and we always will," Beth finished. She looked across the table at Tom. "Promise me you'll bring the family to our new place for a holiday when we get settled?"

"Yes, Beth. I promise." Tom grinned.

Grace stared at her stoic friend. She was tough, caring, and honest—and her loyalty to Tullagulla and those who lived here had been fierce.

"Bronte and Cameron will get a surprise when they return," Grace said.

Tom cleared his throat. "Perhaps. I think Cameron knows how much Greg has struggled since the accident with the bull though—even joked with him recently about retiring. None of us want to see Greg hurt again, and you know we all wish only the very best for you both," Tom added.

Beth chuckled and got to her feet. "Righto, me dears, I'm off home to organise something for my man's lunch. See you later," she said, and shuffled out the door.

Grace waited until her friend disappeared behind the honeysuckle vine before she spoke. "How do we replace them, Tom?"

"Perhaps this is the time to look at alternatives? It gives us the opportunity to think about our long-term plan for Tullagulla—as well as the future of those of us who want to live here."

Grace smiled at her husband. "I'm going out to sit under the cedar tree for a while. Bronte will be back with the kids any minute and then our peace will be shattered."

Tom held her face between his hands as he kissed her. He smelled of wool, sunscreen and traces of shampoo. "Good idea. I'm off to feed the sheep. See you in a couple of hours," he said softly.

He pulled on his boots, reached for his hat, and walked towards the gate. Grace filled a glass with cold water and wandered outside to the coolest place in the garden.

"What do you think, Jane?" Grace spoke aloud as she faced the headstone of Jane McLeod, Tullagulla's first European female resident. "You don't have to answer," she said and grinned.

After pulling the chair closer to the trunk of the tree, she sat facing the breeze, allowing its gentle fingers to lift the hair off her neck, evaporating the ever-present perspiration. It was always hot in summer. But, with the worsening drought, the temperatures had soared, and this year seemed especially scorching to Grace—exacerbated by her internal heater. She sighed and rubbed her stomach as the baby kicked and squirmed.

"Not long now, little one. In the meantime, what are we going to do about Greg and Beth's last Christmas at Tullagulla?"

Grace lay her head against the back of the chair while she mulled over the news. Her initial panic eased, her stomach and the baby relaxed while her mind wound into top gear. Greg and Beth deserved a district farewell party. They had lived out here so long. Most friends from their early years on Tullagulla had moved as many surrounding properties were sold to bigger conglomerates or divided and settled by new families.

Grace doubted that they would agree to anything bigger than a Tullagulla send-off.

A car door slammed, and Grace woke from her reverie and glanced towards the gate.

"Hi. Can I join you?" Bronte smiled as she approached.

"As if you need to ask. Where are Cameron and the kids?"

"I sent the children to get changed. They were a bit wet."

Grace raised her eyebrows.

"Water fight." Bronte chuckled. "Cameron caught sight of Tom loading hay, so he's gone to help him."

The previous evening had been the pony club Christmas party, and Bronte and Cameron had kindly offered to return to the hall to help clean up, leaving Grace to rest and Tom to do the daily feed run.

"I passed Squire heading into town," Bronte said. "Off to visit Lou again I suppose?" Her smile turned to a frown as her eyes met Grace's.

"What's up? You look preoccupied." Bronte's soft English skin was flushed, no doubt from the heat of the afternoon, and her thick, dark curls had escaped the confines of her hair tie. Perspiration trickled down her face, and she wiped it away with her sleeve.

"Greg and Beth are retiring and leaving Tullagulla."

Bronte stared at Grace, her eyebrows raised over vivid blue eyes. "When?"

"Not for another month or so. We knew they'd want to retire before too long, but it seems their visit to the doctor and time spent with their daughters must have hurried things along."

"Wow. I somehow envisaged them being here forever."

"I know. Me too."

A family of blue fairy wrens flitted in and out of the plumbago hedge and drank from the birdbath nearby.

Bronte dragged a chair closer to Grace and sat.

"I'm sure they both have their own doubts and worries about leaving, but they've given Tullagulla a fair innings and we have to respect their wishes. They've had a few health wake-up calls, and Beth said they would like to move closer to their girls, especially now their first grandchild is on the way," Grace said.

"Fair enough. I guess they've saved enough to buy their own house by now?"

"Yes. They've already bought a place. In Tin Can Bay."

"Oh? Where's that?"

"On the coast—about fifty kilometres from Gympie. I went there years ago with Mum and Dad, but I can't remember much about it except it's quiet and has tame dolphins that visit each morning to be fed. It will be much closer for their family, and they'll enjoy fishing and getting involved with the community."

"Sounds like a nice place." Bronte's eyes lit up. "Hey, I have some news."

Grace studied her friend and raised her eyebrows. "I hope it's good?"

"Yeah. I think it is anyway." Bronte paused, her face soft and dreamy.

"Okay, spit it out."

"You know Cameron and I went to see Suzie the celebrant a month or so ago?"

"I may be pregnant but my memory still works from time to time," Grace retorted wryly, and Bronte laughed.

"Well, we bumped into her on our way to the hall. She said she's received approval of the paperwork we need to marry—but get this, she's moving to Perth in January."

"Oh no! Does that mean you have to find someone else?"

Bronte shook her head. "No, it means we have to get moving and organise a wedding before she leaves." Bronte chuckled and clasped her hands together.

Grace studied her vibrant friend. Bronte glowed with health—her glossy curls bounced as she spoke, while her tall, shapely figure was well muscled. The physical lifestyle suited her.

"You know what? I think we should make this Christmas extra special—forget the drought and cheer everyone up. We could invite friends and family here and have a combined farewell for Greg and Beth, and a Christmas get-together. Then seeing as the guests would be pretty much the same people, we could invite them to stay on for your wedding on Boxing Day? Or maybe the day after? What do you think?" Grace asked.

Bronte tilted her head to one side. "That could

work. Cameron's not keen on having a big wedding anyway, and apart from the celebrant, his parents, and our lovely neighbours Alan and Tess, all the people I would want to join us already live on Tullagulla." She laughed. "Oh, except for your parents. Do you think they'll come?"

"Try and keep them away. They'll bring their caravan and stay until the baby's talking to them if they have any say in the matter," Grace said.

"Mu-um!" Daniel's call pierced the air, and they smiled at each other.

"Looks like we need to make a decision fast. What do you think?" Grace asked.

Bronte's smile widened. "Let's do it."

CHAPTER 2

Grace knocked on the door and called, "It's only me.'

Beth's head popped around the door frame.

"Hello, only me. Come in." She bustled towards Grace, drying her hands on her apron.

"I've got a suggestion."

"Ooh, that sounds interesting. Come and sit in the kitchen. I've got the air con nice and cold while I'm cooking."

Grace followed her into the old-fashioned kitchen and sat on a chair. "It's about Christmas. And yours and Greg's farewell."

Beth screwed up her nose. "We don't want a farewell. It's too final … and too sad. We just want to have dinner with you all like we always do on a Friday night, then drive off on Saturday."

"I understand. But please, listen to what I have to say?"

The older lady huffed and plonked herself on the chair opposite Grace.

Within half an hour, Grace's suggestions had Beth twittering with excitement.

The phone rang for what seemed like ages. Grace was on the verge of hanging up when her call was answered.

"Hello." The voice at the end of the line was high and breathless, as if its owner had just run a marathon.

"Is that you, Tess?" Grace asked. It didn't sound like the neighbour she knew.

"Yes, Grace. It's me."

"Are you okay?"

"Of course I am. Just a bit flustered. I was mowing and am seriously pissed off, so I was whizzing around a touch more aggressively than usual," Tess said. "I'd stopped for a drink of water and heard the phone, and ran to answer it—not something I do much anymore."

Grace chuckled in spite of her concern. She'd not witnessed a frustrated Tess before.

"So what's pissed you off?" Grace said.

"The boys."

Grace grinned ruefully. Tess and Alan's boys were both young men now and studying in Brisbane. Their eldest, Dylan, was in his final year, while Scott had begun an Agronomy degree. She had only met Dylan once. However Scott was a familiar face, having spent a year working on the family property after finishing boarding school. He had helped out Tullagulla on several occasions, particularly with harvesting and building the new fences.

"What have they done now?"

"They're off to Japan for a skiing holiday over the Christmas break, so all my plans have been thwarted."

Thwarted? Grace chuckled.

"Friends from Sydney were supposed to be coming up and now they can't, then Alan's dad rang to say he's changed his mind and is going to Alan's sisters for Christmas. Now the boys have announced their trip— so it looks like it'll just be us for Christmas. You know how much we love having a crowd."

Grace grinned. The district stalwart, Tess was the epitome of propriety whether it be organising functions, driving farm vehicles, or helping with the shearing, and Grace envied her. Perhaps good news would cheer her up.

"I'm pleased to hear that, Tess," Grace said. There was silence.

"Why?"

"Because we're having a three-day celebration on Tullagulla. We're starting with Christmas Day, then having a barbecue on Boxing Day to farewell Greg and Beth. Did you know they're retiring?"

"No, I didn't. Although I'm not really surprised. They've had a tough few years and Greg hasn't looked well since the bull got him. So, what's the third day of celebration?"

"Bronte and Cameron's wedding."

"Oh, that's wonderful." Tess's voice bubbled, her disappointment seemingly having evaporated. "Are they having Suzie as their celebrant?"

"Yes, they are. She did such a lovely job at our wedding, and apparently she's heading off to Perth. So this will probably be her last function out our way, at least for a while anyhow."

"Wonderful."

"So, shall I put you down as a yes to all three days?"

"Absolutely. I'll see if Suzie would like to come and stay here. It's time she and I had a good catch up anyway. Haven't seen her for ages."

"She's welcome to join us for all celebrations if she's not doing anything."

"Righto—I'll let you know. Oh, I'll have to buy a new outfit."

Grace smiled at Tess's comment and finished the call. *A new outfit?* Tess always managed to appear well-groomed—even when she was stacking hay bales. Her blonde hair never slipped out of its confines like Grace's did, nor was it wild and unruly like Bronte's—and her work shirts seemed to remain unstained and immaculate.

Grace grimaced and looked down at her old shirt stretched tightly across her belly. *What on earth will I wear?*

CHAPTER 3

The fans and air conditioning were already on full speed as the residents of Tullagulla trooped into the kitchen for their regular Monday morning meeting. Bronte placed a strawberry and almond cake on the table while Beth took the lid off her slice container.

"Morning all," Tom said as he poured the final cup of tea.

Chairs scraped as Squire then Greg took their seats. Grace rested her legs on the stool under the table then shoved a cushion behind the small of her back and wriggled into a comfortable position. The oppressive heat was wearing her down, not to mention she had forgotten how tiring and awkward the final weeks of pregnancy could be.

"Let's start with the farm update first," Tom said. He glanced at the spreadsheet in front of him. "Good news is the perimeter fencing is complete. Thanks, everyone.

Hopefully that will put an end to the needless killing and maiming of the sheep and calves. Squire, you mentioned there have been no more wild dog sightings for several weeks now. Do you think you could pull back on the night inspections and have more time to yourself?"

The creases at the corners of Squire's eyes deepened, and the glimmer of a smile touched his mouth. "Happy to. By the time I feed up and check the bores and dams, there's not much left of the day." His forehead crinkled, accentuating the dividing line between the pale and the deeply tanned skin where his hat usually sat. He stroked his beard. "I think it's time to shift the sheep out of the dam paddock and bring them closer to home. The water level's very low, and we'll have stock getting bogged if we're not careful."

"Good idea. There's still feed left in The Pinnacle paddock, and it's big enough to hold all the ewes and lambs. We can shift them tomorrow." Tom turned to Greg and asked, "What do you think about the cattle?"

Greg opened his mouth, took a deep breath, and in his slow drawl replied, "The calves have done well in spite of the drought. I suggest we sell off a truckload before conditions get any worse."

"I agree," Grace chipped in. "Bronte and I took the kids to the big dam for a swim the other day, and I was surprised how good the young cattle look. If we sell now while the prices are on the rise, at least we won't have to worry. One day it will rain again."

Greg grunted and nodded. "It's not looking promising."

"I know, but we have to hope for the best," Grace said brightly.

"Yep—and prepare for the worst," Tom added.

The farm discussion continued for a further ten minutes, and Bronte got up to make a fresh pot of tea.

"Now for the good news," Grace announced. She waited until Bronte had sat again and began. "Bronte and I have decided that we all need some cheering up—so our suggestion is to have a really special and long Christmas this year before Greg and Beth leave and the baby arrives."

"And what exactly will that entail?" Squire smiled indulgently at Grace and Bronte.

"We thought we'd have a three-day break from all but the essential farm work. On Christmas Day, we can have our traditional dinner with the usual trimmings including games and an afternoon nap." She paused and looked around the table before continuing. "On Boxing Day, we'll have a celebratory barbecue especially devoted to Greg and Beth—and their family of course. Beth's digging out old slides and photos that have been taken here over the years. So we can sit in the air conditioning and relive the history of not just Tullagulla, but Beth and Greg's life here as well. Luckily they've still got their ancient slide projector, which apparently still works." She chuckled. "Then on the twenty-seventh of December, the grand finale will be Bronte and Cameron's wedding—probably in the woolshed just like mine and Tom's." She glanced at each of them, seeking approval —and her grin spread.

"Sounds good to me," Squire said.

Beth clapped and smiled.

"That'll work," Greg said. "I'm pleased you're not going to make us go to the hall and have a big district shindig. Beth knows I hate those things."

Beth caught Grace's eye. "Told you so, didn't I?"

"I think it's a great idea. It's been a hard year—actually, it's been a hard few years. So it will be good to ignore the heat and dry for a spell and enjoy life," Tom said.

"I've already spoken to our girls, and they're coming. Hayley and Nick won't be here until Boxing Day as they're having Christmas with Nick's family. Kirstie will drive out as soon as she finishes work and stay until after New Year. It'll be wonderful to be together again." Beth clasped her hands and rested her chin on them, her elbows on the table. Her round, pink face shone with contentment.

"And I've spoken to Tess. She's very excited and is inviting Suzie, the celebrant, to stay with them over the break. They'll all join in for the three days," Grace said.

"So who else?" Squire asked.

"Grace's mum and dad, Cameron's parents—and of course Lou will be here." Bronte smiled at her father as she spoke. It was no secret that in the past four months, Squire had made more visits to town than he had in the previous twenty-five years—and whenever Lou had days off, she made a beeline for Tullagulla, staying for as long as possible before her next shift at the hospital.

"Sounds like a good crowd. Plenty big enough for us anyway," Greg said dryly.

While Bronte packed the dishwasher, Grace walked out to the gate with Beth. The men were still hovering on the veranda, making plans for mustering.

Grace turned and smiled as Min came galloping towards her. The kelpie had adjusted to having only three legs so well that the missing limb was barely noticeable. When she ran, her gait was as smooth as Tweed and Mollie's with their four legs. Hopping along behind her was Willow, the Eastern Grey kangaroo, now Min's firm friend and companion. Grace bent to pat them both. Willow loved her chest being rubbed and clasped Grace's hand in her two little paws. Min seemed to prefer having Grace's hand rest on her shoulders or stroke her ears.

"Aren't they a lovely pair? I'll miss them," Beth said.

Her voice was wistful, and Grace thought she understood why. *Perhaps Beth is not as keen to leave as she thought she was?* "They are. You and Greg might be able to get a dog once you're settled in your new house."

The women gazed at each other for a few seconds before Beth reached out and hugged Grace. "I'm not upset about leaving. I know the time is right. I guess I'm just a bit uncertain about this next stage of our lives."

Grace released her friend and stepped back, her hand still firmly in Beth's. "I know. It's a big change for you both. But you deserve a rest, and it will be nice to be close enough to your family to see them every week if you want to."

Beth squeezed Grace's hand before dropping it. "Yes, you're right. I keep swinging back and forth from excitement to being afraid of the change. What if we don't like it there? It's one thing to enjoy the place for a holiday, but often living there is a different thing altogether."

"If it's not what you were expecting, you can always move again," Grace said. They both looked at each other and laughed.

"Not likely. This moving business is a nightmare," Beth said. "You should see the junk I've got in the cupboards—thirty-six years' worth." She chuckled and waved as she closed the gate under the arching honeysuckle.

Grace wandered back to the veranda with Min and Willow following. The men were still in deep conversation, and she smiled at them as she opened the door and stepped into the blessedly cool kitchen.

Bronte was chopping tomatoes and cucumber for a salad.

"You're organised. After that lovely cake, I won't be looking for lunch for ages," Grace said.

"Cameron will be though—you and I might not be very hungry, but I know him. He and Alan are preg-testing the last of the Orden Downs cows this morning." She slid the chopped vegetables onto the bed of lettuce and continued. "I thought I'd pre-prepare it so we can nip down to the woolshed. I suspect it will be very dusty, and I want to see how much work will be involved to get it shipshape for the wedding."

"Not much point doing anything this early. We've got nearly three weeks, and another layer will be all over it by then if we don't get rain soon," Grace said despondently.

"Yeah, I know. Well, let's check out Pepperina Cottage then. I haven't been down to give it a clean since that last dust storm came through."

"Bronte, what am I going to do without you?"

"What are you talking about? I'm not going anywhere."

"Yes, you are. You're marrying Cameron, whose surgery is in town, so he'll want you to live with him there won't he?" Grace had been dreading Bronte leaving—especially when the baby was so close and Grace would need her more than ever. A shiver of guilt ran through her. She had deliberately not questioned Bronte about their wedding day, secretly hoping they would continue with the current arrangement of Cameron coming to Tullagulla whenever he could for as long as possible.

"Grace don't worry about it. Cameron and I were planning to talk to you and Tom yesterday, but he was called to help Alan." She paused and retied her hair in a ponytail. "You remember the vet he bought the practice off—Duncan?"

Grace inclined her head questioningly.

"Well, he's not enjoying retirement as much as he

thought he would and has asked Cameron if he could come and help at the surgery from time to time. Cameron really prefers the large animals, and as you know, he's out on properties much more frequently than he is in town. So ... we were wondering if we could move in to Pepperina Cottage after we're married? Then Cameron could work from here and leave Duncan and Theresa, the locum, to manage the surgery. He would still go in whenever he could, of course, but basically they would do the town vet work and he would continue to manage the large animal stuff out on properties. The two nurses are really good and very reliable."

Grace stared at her.

"That's a perfect solution. To be honest, I thought you'd want to leave Tullagulla—and I didn't want to think about it. Especially now that Beth's leaving as well," Grace said.

Bronte clasped Grace's hands in hers, meeting Tom's eyes as he stepped into the kitchen.

"What's happening here? You both look very happy."

"We are. We've been discussing where Cameron and Bronte will live. They were thinking of Pepperina Cottage—but I think we can do better than that," Grace said.

Bronte raised one eyebrow. "And ...?"

"Beth and Greg's house."

Bronte's mouth dropped open. "Really?" she squeaked.

"That's a great idea. They won't be moving until after your wedding, but if we clean and organise the shearers' quarters so it's suitable for guests, you and Cameron could live in Pepperina Cottage until their house is ready for you," Tom removed his glasses, pulled out a handkerchief, and proceeded to clean them.

Bronte twisted her mouth and nodded. "That's a good idea. Private too." She chuckled.

"Before you move into Beth and Greg's house, we'll see if Steve can give it a lick of paint and make it more 'yours'. The outside's been redone since the fire, but it's a long time since the inside was updated. We might even be able to put in a new kitchen. What do you think?" He waited, his gaze flicking between Bronte and Grace until Bronte spoke, stuttering as words jammed in her throat.

"I-I am so touched. I-I've never had my own home, and if we live there, I'll be so close. I'll almost be able to hear the baby crying." She stopped and brushed her hand over her eyes. Bronte's voice squeaked as she continued. "Maddy will love being so close to the homestead and Daniel too. It's a perfect solution."

She paused, her eyes fixed on Tom for a moment.

"I can't wait to tell Cameron." Pressing her fingertips together, she turned suddenly. "And Dad. I'm going to nip down and fill him in now." She dashed out the door, leaving Grace and Tom smiling.

∾

Lunch was over and Grace stood at the sink, scraping the plates into the chook bucket. "Now that your accommodation is settled, Bronte, we need to find you a wedding dress—and you and Cameron had better make sure Suzie is onboard with everything," Grace said.

Tom glanced at Cameron and pushed his chair back. "We'll leave you to it." He kissed Grace, picked up his hat, and opened the kitchen door, allowing a hot blast of air to whoosh inside.

Cameron swung Bronte in a circle and plonked her on her feet. Her cheeks flushed pink and hair fell over her face as he took the steps in one leap and raced after Tom.

Grace waited until they drove off before turning back to Bronte. "Once we've finished here, shall we drive down to Pepperina Cottage? We'll put the air con on in both the shearers' quarters and the cottage while we give them a freshen up. You never know—we might get other visitors between now and Christmas," Grace said hopefully.

"Are you kidding? Who on earth would want to come and stay here at this time of year?" Bronte replied.

Grace met Bronte's eyes. "Umm … your future parents-in-law perhaps. Or would you like them to bunk in with you two?"

"Oh, I see your point."

They gathered buckets, a mop, and cleaning products and loaded them into the back of the ute.

The temperature rose as the two of them worked lethargically in the old quarters. Bronte took the dust covers off beds and removed the quilts from underneath.

"Don't put them in the sun!" Grace called. "I don't want them fading."

"It's okay. No need to get your knickers in a knot. I'm just airing them for five minutes—no more."

Grace sighed. "I'm sorry, Bronte. The heat is messing with my head in spite of this ridiculous drive to clean everything."

Bronte laughed. "You're nesting."

"I'm not bloody nesting. I'm cleaning." Grace kneeled and continued scrubbing the soot marks off the old slate hearth, rattled by Bronte's comment.

Behind her, there was laughter in Bronte's muttering. "She's nesting alright."

Grace huffed, rinsed her cloth in the filthy water, and continued.

*D*inner was barely over that evening when the phone rang.

"I'll go," Tom said. He stood and strode to the office, closing the door behind him.

Grace hushed the brewing argument between Daniel and Maddy. "Come on, kids. Tom won't be able to hear with that racket. It's time for a shower and stories now anyway." She looked across the table at Bronte. "My turn tonight."

"Lucky you. I'll be in as soon as I've finished here," Bronte said.

Grace heaved herself to her feet and followed the children along the corridor.

After showers, she sat on Daniel's bed, propped up against a pile of pillows, her legs stretched out in front of her. With an open book on her lap and a child on either side, her voice rose and fell with the pace of the story while the children's attention remained glued to the page, oblivious to Tom's appearance at the door.

Grace looked up and smiled at her husband. "Nearly finished."

"Okay. I'll just say goodnight to these ratbags and fill you in later." He walked towards them and kissed the children. He then brushed his lips against Grace's cheek and whispered, "Got something to tell you."

Her intrigue piqued, she read a little more quickly, finishing the story as Bronte entered.

"Perfect timing," Grace kissed both children and waited while Bronte took her turn.

"You can have a few more minutes to read on your own, and then it's lights out," Bronte led Maddy over to her own bed and tucked her in before following Grace out of the room.

Tom was filling the kettle when they reached the kitchen, and he turned to face them, his face alight. "Guess who that was on the phone."

"No idea. Tell me," Grace said.

"Zac—Lou's favourite silo painting companion."

"Oh, how is he?" Grace asked.

"He's fine, but he's unemployed. Apparently the company he's been working for has been bought out, and they are staffing it with some of their own people. They've laid off most of the old employees."

"Oh, poor Zac. Just when they've spent a good bit of their savings on their wedding too. So I guess Rachael is supporting them both until he finds another job?" Grace said.

"For the moment, however she is on a contract that runs out at the end of this term. You know Zac—he's not one to sit and do nothing. He was ringing to see if they could come up and stay for a while. Apparently our school bus run is for sale. Did you know that?"

"I read something in the newsletter about Jim having health problems, but I didn't realise he would be selling the run," Grace answered.

"I suppose it makes sense to do it now with the summer school holidays just around the corner. Anyway, Zac somehow found out about it and put in a tender. He was notified that he was successful last week and has been organising finance and licensing. Rachael's going to look around for a teaching position in our area. So ... the short story is that they want to know if they can stay in the shearers' quarters or rent Pepperina Cottage."

"That's amazing news. When do they think they'll come up?" Grace asked.

"Straight after Christmas if possible. I told him about our plans and said they're welcome anytime. We haven't negotiated a rental fee yet, but I'll ring him back tomorrow."

"What are you thinking?" Grace said, smiling. "I can see you're planning something."

Tom laughed. "I am actually. With Greg leaving, we'll be without a mechanic. And as you know, neither Squire nor I have a fraction of Greg's knowledge. I was thinking that we could offer Zac and Rachael free rent in exchange for him doing our mechanical work. There is plenty of room for the school bus to live in the shed, and as he would only be driving for four or five hours a day, the rest of the time he could help here."

Grace reached up and kissed her husband. "You're a good man, Tom Lansdowne. No wonder I married you." She giggled and looked at Bronte.

Quiet and solemn, a stab of concern pierced Grace.

"What's the matter, Bronte?"

"Oh, nothing. It's just, I thought Cameron and I were staying in Pepperina Cottage until Greg and Beth's house was ready for us?"

"Of course you are," Tom said. "Zac and Rachael can live in the shearers' quarters. It's a good thing we renovated last year, and it makes sense to have our facilities used for more than the few weeks a year that shearers need them."

Bronte grinned and clasped her hands.

"It's all happening, Bronte. Tomorrow morning, we'll put the kids on the school bus and head into town to buy you a dress."

"What are you going to wear, Grace? You'll be my bridesmaid, naturally."

"Whatever fits me, I guess. I'm sure we'll find something."

Bronte's excitement was contagious, and Grace rushed into the office, returning with a pen and paper. "Here you go. You're the planner—let's begin."

Rifling through the rack of dresses, Grace had a sense of déjà vu. It had been on one of Bronte's first forays into this little town, that she helped Grace find her wedding dress.

This time, however, their visit to the shop where Grace had bought her outfit was met with disappointment. With only one other boutique that carried formal clothing, they discovered the wedding dresses were either too elaborate or too expensive for Bronte.

"I'm starving. Let's go and have lunch and then we can think about what we do next," Grace said.

She thanked the sales assistant and led Bronte outside, the furnace-hot air blasting their faces as they left the air conditioning. They gratefully slumped onto the colourful café chairs and studied the chalkboard.

Grace pulled a plastic card out of her purse and handed it to Bronte. "Can you order me the Thai chicken salad and a strawberry milkshake please? Get whatever you want and put it on the card. I'm too pooped to stand in the queue."

Bronte took the card and stood at the counter.

After giving their order, she returned as Grace announced, "It looks as though we might have to go to Toowoomba."

Before Bronte could answer, they were distracted by a screaming child on the footpath outside. The mother caught Grace's eye and shrugged helplessly.

"I'm glad we're past that stage," Bronte said.

"Me too. I guess I'll be going through it all again

before long though," Grace said cheerfully. She stroked her belly and spoke quietly. "And I don't even mind."

Bronte grinned and put her elbows on the table. She rested her chin in her hands and took a deep breath. "I really don't want to have to drive to Toowoomba," she said. "I can't believe I used to love shopping in England. Now I don't exactly dislike it, but it doesn't give me the buzz it used to."

"I know. When you live on a farm, pretty dresses and fancy tops just don't cut it. It's the practical, hard-wearing gear that fills my wardrobe these days."

The waitress arrived and placed the food in front of them. "You two look a bit glum. Ruined plans?" she asked.

"Are we that transparent? We're supposed to be shopping for a wedding dress—not very successfully," Bronte said.

The waitress locked eyes with them and squinted. "How do you feel about pre-loved clothing?"

"You mean second-hand stuff?" Grace asked.

"Yeah. That new shop down the side street behind the supermarket has some really nice clothes, and all a fraction of the original price. Worth checking out, I reckon," she said as she turned and walked away.

Bronte watched her go then looked at Grace. "Nothing to lose I suppose?"

Grace nodded and chewed a mouthful of food.

Half an hour later, they stood outside the shop, staring at the bright orange and purple sign hanging above the door—*Penny's Pre-loved Clothing*. Grace dropped her gaze to the clothes in the window. The waitress had been right. Classy, different, and looking like new, the racks of colour drew them inside to be greeted by an attractive woman of an indeterminate age.

"Can I be of some help, ladies?" she asked.

"I don't suppose you have any wedding dresses?" Bronte asked.

"As a matter of fact, I do. Not many, but the selection is growing. Which of you is the bride to be?"

Grace smiled and pointed to Bronte. "She is. I'm the bridesmaid. Although I really don't know what I'm going to wear with this bump to accommodate."

"You sit down, dear." The assistant pointed to a tiny sofa in the corner, and Grace lowered herself into the squishy seat. *I hope I can get out of this again.*

The assistant glided towards the curtain at the rear of the shop. "I haven't had a chance to display all the long dresses yet, so I'll nip out the back and bring some in to show you."

While the woman was away, Bronte fingered the garments on the side wall, removing each one that caught her eye off the rack, studying it, and putting it back again. Grace kicked her sandals off her swollen feet as the assistant returned.

"Here you are. I believe these two are around your size. What do you think?"

In one hand she held a white, strapless dress with a full skirt, and in the other, a soft ivory gown completely covered in dainty patterned lace. Lined with satin, it featured a high neckline and capped sleeves. It was old-fashioned—true vintage—and Bronte's eyes sparkled.

"That's gorgeous. Is it old, or does it just look it?"

"It is more than fifty years old but has been stored well and is in good condition. I believe brides would have traditionally worn long gloves with a style like this. Would you like to try it on?" she asked and slipped it off the hanger.

Bronte followed her to the dressing room while Grace stretched out her legs, shuffling over to soak up the cold air streaming from the split system above the clothing racks.

The dressing booth curtain opened and Grace's eyes widened. "Wow. Bronte, you look beautiful."

"You'd think it was made for her, wouldn't you?" the assistant said.

Bronte beamed and turned to the mirror, fingering the delicate lace while she twisted slowly one way then the other. "I'll take it."

The assistant glanced towards Grace with a smile. "I love decisive customers." She turned back to Bronte. "Would you like a veil? I only have one, but it's old and very soft. It would go well with this dress."

Bronte looked at Grace and shrugged. "What do you think? Should I wear a veil?"

"You can wear whatever you like—it's your wedding. Try it on and see how it looks."

Once again the assistant glided out the back and returned with what appeared to be a handful of gossamer voile. She allowed it to unravel and pinned the fine, gathered band into the back of Bronte's hair. Like an intricate web, it hung in a curtain down her back, reaching below her knees.

Bronte stared quizzically at Grace, and the assistant turned to each of them before speaking. "I will include the veil with the dress at no cost. It looks too perfect on you to ignore."

Bronte beamed and did a final swivel in front of the mirror. "It's beautiful. Thank you."

"Now, what can we find for you to wear?" the assistant said to Grace.

She rifled through the rack and pulled out a dress covered with a tiny floral print in pastel shades of blue, lemon, and a hint of pink.

"I know this doesn't look much on the hanger because the fabric is so soft, but I believe it will suit you perfectly," she said.

Grace struggled to her feet and picked up her sandals. She followed the assistant to the dressing booth and allowed her to help her change. Grace was surprised by the woman's instinct. It did look pretty on her, hanging softly over her belly and almost reaching her ankles. Tiny buttons opened down the front, and she smiled. "This will be handy after the baby arrives too—if I have any occasion to wear it afterwards, at least I'll be able to feed bub without having to strip off."

The assistant helped her remove it before carefully wrapping the dresses and veil.

"Well, that was a surprise," Grace said as they climbed into the car.

"Not to mention a relief." Bronte grinned.

"Wait until Cameron sees you in that dress—and Squire. They will be over the moon with pride," Grace said. "What shall we do about flowers? It's going to be a bit tricky trying to buy some right on Christmas and in this heat."

"We don't need to buy any. I want to use the Tullagulla flowers—like you did. The honeysuckle's still flowering, and Mum's rose bush has never looked better. That's all I want."

"Perfect. Do you want to drop me off at the medical centre and go and sign those documents with Cameron? I'll wait in the air conditioning until you finish," Grace said.

As Grace stepped out of the heat and into the doctors cool reception area, she breathed a sigh of relief.

Grace smiled at the screen as the baby kicked and squirmed.

"Do you want to know the gender?" The doctor glanced at Grace.

"No. I don't think so. I'll be happy to have a healthy baby and I don't mind if it's a girl or a boy."

He moved the probe around her stomach again before replying.

"That's lucky because today this little one is being very coy and not allowing us to have a clear view." As he wiped the gel from her tummy, he asked, "Have you decided on any names yet?"

"Yes, but we're not telling anyone in case we change our minds when we meet the baby."

The doctor nodded. "Very sensible. Have you any other questions or concerns?"

"Only that I don't remember feeling this tired and clumsy during my last pregnancy. Am I being a princess?"

He smiled and patted her hand.

"No, you're not. I can't give you a definitive answer but I can reassure you that everything is proceeding as it should. It has been an exceptionally hot summer and you're older than when you had Daniel which can make a difference."

"I suppose so."

"Could it be possible that you are doing too much?"

Grace met his gaze and grinned.

"Hmm, possibly."

He chuckled and shook his head.

"I thought as much. Go home and rest."

As Grace walked back into the reception area, she sighed.

Rest? What does that really mean?

CHAPTER 5

*A*rriving at the stop seconds behind the bus, Grace let the wind whistle through her teeth. "Phew. That was good timing."

"Yeah—don't ask me to be your co-driver in a car rally," Bronte said.

Grace grinned at her. "Don't you dare let on to Tom that I drove that fast. He'd have fifty fits."

Bronte drew her thumb and forefinger over her closed lips. "Your secret's safe with me, girlfriend."

The car door was reefed open and Daniel shoved his school bag on the floor. As he and Maddy climbed into their seats, Bronte got out to fasten their belts, and Maddy waved an envelope under her mother's nose. "This is the notice about our end of year thingy. You have to come to school to help the ladies make our costumes."

"I told Mrs Taylor you can't sew, Mum. So you don't need to come," Daniel said.

"Thanks for your confidence, mate." Grace pursed her lips and glanced in the rear view mirror. "I can sew. You just haven't seen me make anything since Bronte's been with us because she does it for us. Anyway, what has to be sewn?"

"Our costumes for the Christmas concert," Daniel said, his puzzled tone carried a hint of reprimand.

Grace grimaced. Had she forgotten? She had no recollection of having been asked to help. She dismissed it and replied, "What are the costumes?"

"Us kids in Prep and year one are sheep and cattle. Abigail gets to be Mary, and Tim is Joseph. Mum, can you have the baby this week so it can be baby Jesus?"

Grace chuckled. "Sorry, mate. Babies come when they're ready to, and this one has a little while to go yet. Perhaps Maddy could take her dolly to school and see if Mrs Taylor would be happy with that?"

"I don't want to be a sheep. I want to be the donkey." Maddy pouted.

"But, sweetheart, donkeys have to be very strong, and you need one of the big kids for that. Remember the donkey had to carry Mary a long way to get to Bethlehem?" Bronte replied.

"Oh. I still don't want to be a sheep." She huffed and sat back in her seat, folding her arms across her chest.

"We're going to be very busy getting ready for Christmas now, so Grace and I will need you both to help us," Bronte said.

"Why?" Daniel asked.

"Because we've got lots of activities at school next

week, then we'll have to find a Christmas tree and decorate it—and then we've got to get ready for Beth and Greg's farewell party, and then there's the wedding. Nanny and Poppy are coming to stay. And Lou, and Alan and Tess," Grace said.

Daniel grinned and Maddy clapped. "Can I wear my pretty dress to the wedding, Mum?"

"Of course." She glanced at Grace and rolled her eyes.

They drove over the Tullagulla grid and the conversation stilled. The fluttering in Grace's belly grew and she swallowed. Was it the baby? Or had she bitten off more than she could chew. Three consecutive days of celebration already had a ring of exhaustion to it, and it hadn't even begun.

Grace sat in the office with her feet on a stool and the air conditioning on the coldest setting. She totalled the columns on the spreadsheet and sighed. The losses in the last six months had been much greater than any other since Tom took over Tullagulla. Fencing out feral animals had been a huge expense—but it had been worth it.

She looked down at Min curled up in her bed. What they really needed now was rain. Not just a shower, but good, soaking rain that went on for hours—and was repeated a week later. *Stop dreaming.*

She pushed herself to her feet and waddled to the

kitchen for another glass of cold water. The house was silent. Bronte was at school with the children and would return with them after a day of costume making. And in addition to the never-ending rounds of feeding stock, Tom and Squire were building new yards behind the stables.

Grace paused. She had forgotten to ask them why they needed new yards there. *My memory is worse than I thought.*

She picked up the remote and turned the kitchen television on. Slumping into the sofa, her concentration intensified as the map of Australia covered the screen and the weather announcer pointed to a tropical low forming in the ocean off Western Australia. *At least someone might be lucky enough to get some rain for Christmas.*

She returned to the office and picked up the phone. "Hi, Mum. How're things?"

"Great. Better than you sound anyway. Are you alright?"

"Yes. Just fat, hot, and tired," Grace said.

Her mother chuckled. "I know, love. Summer pregnancies are tough, but not long to go now," Margot said cheerfully. "Your problem is you don't sit down long enough to rest."

"Yes I do. I've been sitting down all morning doing the bookwork."

"I thought Tom did the books?"

"He does, usually. The men are busy feeding and constantly moving stock though, to avoid overgrazing.

They're also drafting the cattle and selling whatever is ready. I told him the least I could do was to catch up with the paperwork."

"Fair enough. You don't sound yourself, love."

Neither spoke for a couple of seconds.

"I'm fine, Mum, honestly. I just got a bit of a shock at how high our costs have become with this drought. We're lucky Tom took on a partner in the Melbourne office. Even though he hasn't had much opportunity to fly down recently, at least he gets an off-farm income. If we get too hard up, he'll just have to go back to it."

"Hmm. Dad and I were thinking of coming up earlier than usual this year. The boys and their families have made other plans, so we're getting together with them on Saturday to celebrate Christmas early. Then we'll hook on the caravan and head up to you. How does that sound?"

"Oh, Mum. It would be absolutely fantastic." Grace choked on her words. "I don't remember being this emotional when I was expecting Daniel, and now I have a loving, caring husband who dotes on me. Nothing like last time when you and Dad were virtually my only support. Remember Pete wouldn't even let me talk about it?"

Her mother cleared her throat as a shiver ran down Grace's back. Pete's disinterest in the child he had conceived with Grace was something she would never forget.

"Don't worry, love. I'm sure everything will be fine.

We'll see you soon—in plenty of time for the kids' end of year activities."

Grace lay on the sofa. The clock ticked in the silent homestead, and she flicked the television back on. A movie played and her mind drifted, staring unseeing at the screen until the baby kicked hard. She jumped.

"Alright, little one. Are you restless too? Let's go and see how Beth and Greg are getting on."

She slipped her bare feet into her sand-shoes and pulled her Akubra down to shade her eyes. Min was at her heels before she opened the door.

A whirly wind blew dust across the track and through the eucalypts, rustling the leaves as it travelled. The corrugated iron on the shed roof crackled in the heat and Grace glanced at the hazy sky as a flock of screeching galahs flew overhead. Brushing the sweat from her face, she crossed the dry, brown lawn that surrounded Greg and Beth's house and trudged up the steps onto the shaded veranda.

"Hi, Beth. It's only me," she called as she knocked.

"Welcome to the shambles," Beth retorted.

Grace grinned as she cast her gaze around the room. Boxes were stacked on top of one another in the corner, and bubble wrap and newspaper laid on the table, weighted down with scissors and a roll of tape.

"I decided to wash all our good china and pack it away now so that when we get to our new house, we can just open the boxes and put everything straight into the cupboards. The girls will help us with their bedrooms when they get here, but I would like to be as organised as possible before then," Beth said.

"Good idea," Grace glanced out the window. "Where's Greg?"

"In the garage. He doesn't have many tools of his own—as you know, they mostly belong to Tullagulla. But over the years, he's bought a few bits and pieces, so he's tidying them up and cleaning the shed. I think his fishing gear is the most important thing to him." She laughed. "Feel like a cold drink?"

"Love one. Thanks. Shall I go out and get Greg?"

"He'll be in any minute, no doubt. Sit yourself down."

"The kids were wondering if you would both like to come to the school concert next Thursday? They're having it at eleven-thirty, and parents are asked to bring a plate of food to share for lunch. I think after that we're allowed to take the kids home."

"Of course, we'd love to," Beth said. "Is that the last day of school?"

"Sort of. It's officially open on Friday, but the staff are encouraging the children to stay home if they want to. They will be cleaning up and then heading off themselves from what I can gather."

Beth nodded and poured them both a glass of iced water.

"Mum and Dad are coming up early next week as well, maybe even on Sunday. They said they'll be here in time for the concert and can stay until after the baby is born—and, knowing Mum, for a couple of weeks after that." Grace chuckled.

"Ooh, it's getting exciting now isn't it? Christmas is just around the corner, then the wedding. All we need now is some rain," she finished as the back door opened, allowing a blast of hot air to enter along with her husband.

"It'll rain soon. Just wait and see." Greg's voice interrupted as he hung up his hat and sat at the table.

"I hope you're right. The only hint of anything over the whole continent is a front off the coast of Western Australia. I can't imagine that will get this far, even if it does eventuate in rain," Grace said quietly.

Greg had not regained any of the weight he had lost following his accident, and his skin had a saggy appearance. His round, kind face, with the patch over one eye, now drooped, resembling that of an old bloodhound. The shock announcement of them leaving Tullagulla had rattled her, but Grace accepted it was the right thing for them to do. She would never forgive herself if he didn't enjoy retirement.

"Grace was just telling me school finishes next week, and we're invited to the end-of-year concert. It seems strange knowing this will be our last opportunity to go—so we're not going to miss it," Beth announced fiercely.

Greg nodded, his face gentle and solemn.

Grace studied him for a moment and met Beth's

gaze. She gave a tiny shake of her head and poured his tea.

Is he having second thoughts?

The following two days were consumed in a flurry of mustering and drafting cattle for the final sale of the year. While Bronte helped Squire, Tom, and Greg, Grace did the school run and prepared meals. The sky remained clear and dry, and the temperatures continued to soar.

Grace loaded morning tea into the Land Cruiser and drove to the yards.

"I don't know how you've done this year after year, Grace," Bronte said. She flopped on the sparse brittle grass under a tree and wiped the sweat from her face with her sleeve.

"I guess when I'm not pregnant I don't feel the heat so much—and you know how much I love being outside," she answered languidly. "I'm really grateful you're able to step in."

Bronte grinned and took a bite of Grace's freshly baked chocolate brownie. She crunched it loudly between her teeth and studied the remainder of her piece. "What temperature did you cook these on?"

"Umm—two hundred I think. I sort of forgot about them for a while 'cause I was putting fresh hay in the henhouse." Grace screwed up her face as she attempted to take a bite of the portion in her hand.

The men joined Grace and Bronte under the tree, and Squire picked up a mug of tea and dipped his brownie into the steaming hot liquid. Grace and Bronte looked at each other and grinned.

"I'm not sure that our role reversal is entirely satisfactory if that's the only way my brownies are edible," Grace said, and threw her piece of slice to Min.

Bronte tightened the girth of her saddle and turned to Grace.

"I'll be back to help you with lunch so don't worry too much about it. By the time you've cleaned up this lot and hung out the washing, Dad and I'll have the next mob of cattle here."

Grace shot her a grateful grin. She had completely forgotten about the load of washing, and it was clear her friend suspected as much.

CHAPTER 6

Grace woke with a start. A stab of panic gripped her, and she reached for Tom. His side of the bed was empty. While her fuddled thoughts unscrambled, a truck rumbled closer, changing gears as it neared the homestead. She rolled out of bed and stumbled to the French doors leading from the bedroom onto the veranda. Pale fingers of light broke through shadows in the paddock, and Grace breathed in the heavy scents of soil, manure, and dust. The truck thundered past and continued along the track towards the yards, its empty cattle crates rattling noisily as it went.

The cattle. That's where Tom will be.

She dressed quickly and splashed water on her face. Before crossing the living room, she peeped into the children's bedroom. Both beds were empty. Her forehead creased as she hurried to the kitchen.

"Good morning," Bronte greeted her cheerfully.

"Hi," Grace croaked. "Where are the kids?"

"They went with the men to watch the cattle being loaded."

"Oh, have you had a cuppa?"

"Yes. Sit down and I'll make you one. Tom said it would take about an hour to get the trailers loaded, so you've got plenty of time to put your feet up before they arrive for breakfast."

Grace leaned her head against Bronte's shoulder. "Thanks. You're a lifesaver."

Bronte grinned and gently guided Grace over to the kitchen sofa. She flicked the television on and lifted Grace's feet onto the footstool.

"Is madam comfortable? Would she care for a bowl of fresh fruit salad while I make the tea?" Bronte joked.

"No thanks. Madam would be happy with a cuppa."

Grace's smile died as the weather map on the television consumed her attention. "Looks like that front is moving inland. I hope it brings drought-breaking rain to someone over there."

"Yeah. It's a shame it's not over this side of the country," Bronte replied and handed Grace a mug of raspberry leaf tea.

Grace stared at the contents and smiled. "My favourite. You're a darling, Bronte."

She had barely finished her drink when the children clattered into the kitchen.

"Bronte! Mum! Come and see. Bully Boy wrecked the yards and has escaped!" Daniel yelled.

"Bully Boy?" Bronte threw the tea towel on the bench and frowned.

"Yeah. You know? The one that hurt Greg. Tom put a green ear tag in him and told everyone to be careful and not get in Bully Boy's way." Daniel's eyes grew large and round. "Then Squire yelled at us to get in the ute."

"So how did you get here?" Grace asked.

The screen door onto the veranda opened again and Greg stepped into the kitchen. "With me. Grace, can we leave the kids with you? And could you spare us a few minutes, Bronte?"

"Sure." She rushed to the veranda and pulled on her boots. Slapping her Akubra on her head, she removed a stock whip from the peg on the wall and hurried after Greg.

"We want to watch," Maddy whined.

"I know, sweetheart. But bulls can be very dangerous. You know that's why this one is being sold. We'll watch from the veranda, but we are not going any closer."

Before Maddy could complain, Grace grasped her hand and pulled her through the door.

In the still morning air, a cloud of dust rose from beyond the belt of casuarinas and the crack of whips echoed across the paddock. Men's voices mingled with the bellow of cattle and the clatter of hooves on the steel of the truck floor. Grace's pulse thumped as the ute sped down the track.

For several minutes, the children ran up and down

the veranda while Grace craned her neck, desperate to see what was going on. A galloping horse appeared briefly, its rider leaning forward in the saddle while the crack of a whip sounded again and again. The horse disappeared and seconds later, the slamming of steel on steel sang across the paddock.

Grace stood frozen, her eyes glued to the belt of trees.

"What's happening?" Daniel asked.

"I don't know, love. Hopefully they've rounded him up again and got him into the truck."

They waited.

It was another ten minutes before the rumble of a diesel engine sounded and the green and silver cab pulled onto the track. Hauling two long trailers loaded with cattle, the driver changed gears several times before the truck passed the homestead without stopping.

Grace raised her eyebrows.

"Isn't he staying for breakfast, Mum?"

"It seems not, mate. But the others should be here soon, so we'll go and get it ready."

By the time the rattle of farm utes and the buzz of a motorbike drew near, the children had laid plates and cutlery on the kitchen table, and Grace was cracking eggs. The smell of toast mingled with bacon greeted the dishevelled group of workers arriving.

Tom stepped into the kitchen first, closely followed by Squire, Bronte and lastly, Greg.

"Well, that was a bit of excitement to start our day,"

Tom said, meeting Grace's solemn face with a half-smile.

"Daniel said the bull escaped."

"Yep. We closed the gate behind the cows on the truck and were about to run him up into the section behind them when he went crazy. Jammed his head under the new panel next to the loading ramp and pulled the whole thing off its brackets."

Grace held her hand over her mouth.

"Just as well Squire was on Beau. That old horse just took off after him." Tom laughed. "I swear he must have thought he was back in the campdraft arena."

Grace grinned at Squire and raised her eyebrows.

"I gave a few cracks in the air with the whip and Beau stopped the bugger in his tracks. Once he settled down a bit and realised all his cows were already on the truck, it wasn't difficult getting him up the ramp."

Greg harrumphed. "Huh. It was pretty funny watching the driver after that. He was gunna have breaky with us, but after the campdraft display, I reckon he wanted to get them into the saleyards as quickly as possible."

Grace smiled and exhaled.

Just another day on Tullagulla.

The hot afternoon sun slowly crept towards the western horizon as the rumble of vehicles resonated with the residents on Tullagulla.

"Mum. Nanna and Poppy are here!" Daniel shrieked.

A Land Cruiser towing a caravan rounded the bend and stopped outside the house yard gate. As her mother stepped out of the driver's seat, Grace hurried down the path towards her, pausing as she stepped onto the gravel. "Where's Dad?" Her forehead creased.

"He's coming," Margot answered as a white ute towing a horse float pulled to a halt twenty metres away.

Daniel flew past, closely followed by Maddy, while Tom strode towards Grace and stood next to her. Grace hesitated and her smile vanished. "Why have you come in two vehicles? And why have you brought the horse float?" she asked anxiously.

The children clamoured to hug Margot first while Martin grinned and winked at Tom, confusing Grace even further. She barely felt her mother's hug as a low *moo* sounded from within the float's confines, and her concentration locked on the vehicle. "What's going on?"

"Merry Christmas, love—a little early," Martin beamed.

Her father clasped Grace's hand and towed her gently towards the float. He opened the small access door at the front and stepped back, allowing Grace to peer inside.

She leaned in and then turned back to Tom and her parents, her eyes huge green pools. "Queenie?"

"Yep, sure is. She's all grown up now and milking

well. We thought you could do with a nice house cow, and there's none more suitable than the dear little heifer you reared before you moved here. She's got a four-week-old calf herself and is feeding another one—so we brought you all three!"

Tears pricked Grace's eyes, and a warm glow spread inside her. She smiled at the cow and rubbed her face, while Queenie nudged Grace and gave another soft *moo*.

"My lovely Queenie," Grace whispered. "You're a Mumma now, and you've come to join me on Tullagulla."

Grace backed out of the cramped area and grinned while Daniel and Maddy scrambled inside to pat the calves sitting on a heap of straw next to the cow.

She hugged both her parents before Tom spoke. "I know you didn't think we needed more yards, but now you understand why Squire and I have been busy down there the last few days."

"So you're all in on this?"

Bronte was standing in the shade of the honey-suckle arch with her arms folded. "Not me."

"The calves are a Christmas present for each of the children. They're both little heifers, so the kids can teach them how to lead and be tied up, and all that stuff, and when they're grown, they can be milkers for you all as well." Martin paused as a flicker of concern crossed his face. "So, what do you think?"

Grace laughed. "I think we'd better get the poor girl out if they've all been cramped in there for hours."

"Are you feeling alright love? You look a bit pale."

"I'm fine, Mum."

She grinned and ducked back into the front of the float. She took hold of the lead rope attached to the cow's headstall while Tom and Martin lowered the back ramp. Queenie turned her big black and white head and stamped a hoof.

"You can back off now, girl," Grace said.

She leaned on the cow's shoulder as Queenie took a tentative step backwards, stopped, and sniffed the air. In a rush, she clattered down the ramp, reefing Grace sideways as she went.

"Whoa, girl."

The cow stopped as suddenly as she had started and licked Grace's outstretched hand. Her rough tongue sandpapered her skin and Grace chuckled.

"You remember me, don't you, girl? You used to love licking my hand when you were a baby."

The calves stretched and skipped excitedly out of the float, bellowing. One of them ran in a circle before returning to the cow and joining its friend frantically sucking on her udder.

It was quite a crowd trailing along the dusty track towards the stables and new yards with Grace leading the big Friesian cow while the two calves trotted along beside her. Daniel and Maddy raced ahead and then back to the adults several times with Min at their sides.

Grace rested one hand on the cow's neck, breathing in the familiar, milky scent while happy visions of helping her father in the dairy danced in her memory.

When they reached the stables, Grace's eyes widened. Just out of sight from the homestead, Tom and Squire had built a milking bail and a roomy calf pen. A much larger yard—more like a small paddock—had also been fenced off next to the pony paddock in order to keep both calves and the cow safe while they settled in. A mesh V-shaped rack stood in the middle of the yard overflowing with hay while protected from above by a wide corrugated iron roof and a new trough filled one corner, full of fresh, clean water.

"This is fabulous," Grace said softly. "I don't know how you kept it all a secret from me."

"Let's just say it wasn't easy. Luckily Bronte has been able to occupy you with wedding and Christmas plans," Tom said and shot a grin at Bronte.

Grace slipped the headstall off Queenie and leaned on the railing for a minute while the cow took a long drink from the trough.

Squire stepped from behind the other end of the stables and walked around the outside of the yard to stand against the fence with Grace and the children. "Do you like your Christmas present, Grace?"

"Oh, Squire. I love it. I love everything—especially the amount of organising and work you have all done to make this happen for me." She turned to her parents. "Thanks very much, Dad—and Mum. Even though I know it's easier to buy milk than having to milk a cow, I have missed having one. Shop-bought milk is never quite the same."

"It'll be a completely new experience for me," Bronte chipped in. "But I'll give it a go if someone can teach me how to milk, Grace."

"I'll show you while I'm here, Bronte," Martin said kindly.

"And I can help too," Squire said. "I used to milk cows when I was a boy, and I suppose it hasn't changed much."

"They look pretty happy," Margot said, gazing at the new arrivals. "I don't know about anyone else, but I'm dying for a cup of tea—or something stronger."

"Me too," Martin said. He looked down at his watch. "What do you reckon, fellas—beer o'clock?"

Grace tucked her hand into her father's arm. "Come on then. Perfect timing for a cold drink under the cedar tree."

A gentle breeze fanned their faces, and Grace lifted her hair from her neck and slumped further into her chair. The sun had set, leaving a golden glow over the horizon, and she revelled in the departure of the sticky black flies as darkness fell.

Tom turned on an outside light, while Margot relaxed into the seat next to Grace.

"How are you really, love?" she asked softly.

"I'm good." Grace hesitated for a moment. "I've had a few niggling reminders that I'm pregnant—more than I did with Daniel. But I guess I'm six years older, not to mention living in a much hotter environment than last time."

Margot smiled at her daughter. "I'm glad I'm here."

"Me too." Her eyes glistened as Margot squeezed her hand.

CHAPTER 7

The following morning, Grace and her mother were kept busy in the kitchen. It was cool, and there was a lot to do. Bronte had disappeared to the dining room to sew costumes for the school concert, and strains of Adele filtered down the corridor. Grace finished slicing cabbage for coleslaw, while Margot effortlessly made a large batch of tomato chutney with the oversupply from both her and Grace's gardens.

"This is the last from my veggie patch," Grace said as she tipped half a bucket of tomatoes into the sink. "Since the heat really started to bite in October, I haven't had the water to spare."

She sighed, and Margot shot her a sidewards glance.

"I had to pull the last of the veggies out a fortnight ago and threw what I couldn't salvage to the chooks. At least I managed to save the tomatoes—and we're lucky to have the cold room," Grace finished.

Margot brushed her grey hair from her face. "What about pumpkins? You grew so many last year."

"There are a few coming on, thanks to the leftover water from the washing machine, but none will be ready for Christmas," Grace answered.

Margot rested her hand briefly on Grace's shoulder. "Lucky we came prepared then. Our garden has been wonderful. We haven't had as much rain as usual, but that beautiful, big river is a godsend."

The Clarence River ran alongside most of her parents' farm in northern New South Wales and, until Grace moved to Tullagulla, she had not appreciated the abundance of water she had grown up with. "Any fresh peas?" Grace asked hopefully.

"About three kilos of them. Will that be enough?" Margot grinned and tipped the box towards Grace. It was a sea of green—peas and beans, lettuces, and other vegetables.

Grace chuckled and turned to the bowl of cabbage on the table. She added chopped spring onions, carrots, and apple and stirred in the mayonnaise. "Coleslaw's done. I've got another appointment with the doctor tomorrow. Tom's coming with me. Did you want to join us?"

Her mother had been helpful during and after Daniel's birth—and with Pete's frequent absence and lack of interest, her involvement had been gratefully received. Having Tom at her side during this pregnancy filled her with contentment and anticipation, and a feeling of guilt sat in her stomach. She hoped her mother didn't feel shut out.

"I'll come if you really want me to, but I'm happy to stay put and help Bronte with the costumes and kids. A full day on the road yesterday was enough for me." Margot shrugged apologetically. "I'll be more use to everyone here in the air conditioning." She smiled and poured the chutney into the jars.

Grace chuckled and covered the coleslaw. Peace descended on her like a hug. "It's great to have you here, Mum."

That afternoon, Grace, Bronte, and Margot were joined by Beth as they loaded buckets, mops, and brushes onto the back of the ute and drove to the woolshed.

The sky was a deep blue and the oppressive heat had increased, sending perspiration down everyone's faces, while the ever-present flies stuck to their backs and tried to crawl into their eyes.

Grace walked around the old corrugated iron shed, throwing every window and door open while Bronte connected the hose to the bore water tap outside. Water ran across the wooden floor as they scrubbed and mopped. Beth turned the radio up and sang tune-lessly as she sprayed and rubbed the glass windowpanes.

Almost two hours later, Grace announced, "I'm ready for a break."

She glanced at her watch and sat on a pile of folded wool packs before plunging her feet into a bucket of dirty water.

"Of course, love. We're nearly finished anyway. Shall we set up tables and chairs now?" Margot said.

Grace was grateful for her calm, efficient mother. "I don't think so, Mum. If we get a dust storm between now and the wedding, we'll just have to clean it all again. At least the majority is done and we can concentrate on other things over the next few days. I want Dad to help me outside while you give Bronte a hand with the cooking," Grace said, immediately biting her tongue.

She was being bossy and now regretted it. If Margot was offended, she made no comment and turned to pack up the cleaning equipment.

Grace and Tom crossed the boundary grid as the Subaru slowed and pulled up alongside them.

Lou lowered her window. "Good morning," she called cheerily.

Grace leaned over as Tom opened the driver's window. "You're up early," Grace grinned.

"Hello, Lou!" Daniel and Maddy yelled from the back seat.

"Hi, kids!" Lou called.

"We're dropping the children at the bus stop on our way to town. Bronte's at home with Mum and Dad if you want to call in for a cuppa?" Grace said.

"Thanks. I'd love to meet your parents—and of course spend time with Bronte, but I'll have my riding lesson first before it gets too hot," she explained.

"Enjoy it. We're off to get the last bits and pieces for Christmas and for another doctor's appointment. See you later."

Lou gave them a wave and turned into Tullagulla, while Tom and Grace accelerated away.

"I'm so happy for Squire," Grace said. "After all these years of solitude, he and Lou seem very content together."

Tom reached over and squeezed her hand. "Yes, and I know how pleased you and Bronte are about it all—you're quite the romantic, aren't you?"

She shot him a smile. "We're lucky she's living in Primrose Cottage. Henry would be delighted to know that his garden is being cared for as he would have liked it—and that his cat, Pansy is so content."

Tom shared a smile full of love and adoration before concentrating on the corrugated road ahead.

"I'll see you again next week, Grace," the doctor said.

Grace gave the doctor a half-smile and stood to say goodbye before Tom ushered her out into the hot, still air.

The shopping was done, with the car fridge full of cold items and the back seat covered in gifts, boxes, and bags. Tom held the door of the local pub open and followed Grace into the hotel restaurant. They sat at a table next to a window overlooking the garden, and Grace studied the roses wilting in the hot summer sun, while lavender and salvias stood strong and bright, covered with busy bees.

"This might be our last chance to have a peaceful meal together for quite some time," Tom said. "Let's make the most of it."

Grace put her hand over his. "Are you excited?"

"About the baby, you mean?" He raised his eyebrows. "Yes, very. You know my ex-wife didn't want children, and being an only child myself, I guess I never dared to hope that my dreams of having a family would be realised." He squeezed Grace's hand with both of his and grinned. "And here we are, about to have our baby —and I'm just a tad terrified."

They shared a smile as the waitress came to take their order.

That evening, a gentle breeze blew across the lawn, rustling the leaves of the cedar tree and providing a more pleasant temperature for those sitting outside. Smoke from the wood barbecue drifted away, and the nuisance flies became lethargic as dusk fell.

"Would you all like to come to Allanga with us

tomorrow?" Squire asked. "Lou and I've got something we'd like to show you." There was excitement in Squire's tone that promised more than a check of cattle and fences.

"We'd love to," Grace glanced across at Bronte and raised her eyebrows.

Bronte shrugged. It was clear she was as clueless as Grace. Squire had not owned the property long and had spent most of his spare time replacing fences, installing new water sources, and removing vast swathes of prickly pear. The only structure on the property had been an old timber cattle yard and loading ramp—the first items to be replaced after Squire purchased the land.

"Have you got anything on it yet?" Martin asked.

"Yes. Tom and I put a mob of steers over there to help clean it up. In spite of the drought, there's a surprising amount of feed, and now I'm getting the noxious weeds under control, the pastures should come along quite well … when we next get rain."

Martin nodded thoughtfully. "What about sheep? Is the country suitable for them?"

"That's my aim, although we'll continue to work together—Tom and Grace and I—and until it's cleaned up a bit more, we won't risk moving sheep onto it. Too much vegetable matter."

A spark of excitement warmed Grace. It was weeks, months even, since she and Bronte had accompanied Squire on a drive around Allanga. Her pregnancy and the constant increasing heat had prioritised her time in other ways.

With the children fast asleep, the adults stayed outside enjoying the slightly cooling breeze and talking quietly amongst themselves while a bright moon rose. Almost full, but not quite, it shone its light on the trees and highlighted Tom's Cessna, crouched like a waiting bird on the airstrip.

Squire was the first to make a move, reaching for Lou's hand and helping her to her feet. They said goodnight and turned to wave as they reached the honeysuckle archway. Grace and Bronte followed as far as the kitchen steps, carrying the empty bowls and glasses. Entering the veranda, Grace kicked off her shoes as Lou and Squire's receding figures strolled down the dusty track, their arms around each other's waists. She nudged Bronte and smiled.

"I know. I'm thrilled for them," Bronte said. "If it can't be Mum, I reckon Lou is the next best person to share Dad's life. I love her to bits."

"Me too," Grace whispered. "She was a godsend with the sheep scanning, not to mention Greg's awful accident with the bull. There's no doubt about it—having a nurse around sure is handy." She paused. "And without Lou and Cameron, I wouldn't have Min." Grace looked at the three-legged Kelpie lying on the veranda and smiled as the dog's tail thumped with pleasure under her mistress's gaze.

CHAPTER 8

The day of the Allanga tour was here and Grace and her father rushed through the morning chores. Having milked Queenie and fed the horses, dogs, and chooks, they arrived at the homestead seconds before Bronte returned from the school bus run.

"You'll have to stay home this time, Min. Have a sleep." Grace patted the little dog gently and waved to Squire and Lou as they pulled up behind Bronte's vehicle.

Squire's ute was stacked neatly with eskies and folding chairs, and he leapt out of the driver's seat and followed Bronte inside, returning seconds later with a box of thermos flasks and water containers which he loaded onto the ute tray.

Beth hustled over to the Land Cruiser, tightening the cord of her hat under her chin. Her open shirt flapped in the breeze and sunscreen glistened on her weathered face. "Greg's going with Martin and Tom. Can I come with you girls?"

"Of course, Beth. Hop in," Bronte said and opened the back door.

Beth sat next to Margot, while Grace slid into the front and pulled on her seat belt, squirming to click it into place.

"Are we ready?" Bronte asked.

"Yes," the women chorused. Bronte put the car into gear and followed the utes down the track.

With several stops to check water troughs, it was over an hour before they reached the boundary between Tullagulla and Allanga. They faced a high mesh gate, from which a brand-new fence ran in either direction. Lou stepped out and opened it, waiting until each vehicle had passed through before she swung it closed.

"We're heading to the new yards, so follow us," she said.

A further ten-minute drive over a rough track took them to a set of stock yards with a small corrugated iron shed at one end. Positioned on a slight ridge, they overlooked a wide expanse of native pasture and euca-lyptus trees, while a long, narrow lane edged with a taut ring-lock fence on either side granted access to them.

The vehicles came to a halt, and everyone tumbled out before Squire pointed past the yards to the contin-uing track. "If we'd continued along there for another two kilometres, we'd end up at the gravel road on the western end of the property. That is the official front entrance to the farm."

"It looks lovely, Squire. You've done so much work since I last visited," Grace said.

He grinned and put his arm around Lou's shoulders. "I've had a great offsider. She's a pretty handy assistant."

They gazed at each other, and Grace's heart melted. It wasn't just love that shone between the two of them, but a respect that had obviously grown over recent months—and an element of surprise hit Grace. She had missed the signs.

Must have been more preoccupied than I thought.

"It's wonderful, Dad. No wonder you've been dozing off after dinner," Bronte added.

"That's not all."

Squire and Lou shared a brief smile.

"Back in the vehicles, everyone. Follow me," Squire said.

They trailed after the white ute for another two hundred metres before branching off and travelling along the highest point of the ridge. Once again, Squire stopped and he and Lou stepped out of the vehicle. He pointed in front of them, towards the foot of the rise, and Grace's eyes widened.

Below was a long, thin creek bed that had been excavated and reformed into a series of ponds, divided by barriers of granite and logs. A trickle of water sparkled as it fell over rocks at the head of the gully, pooling in shallow, muddy puddles further along.

"I discovered a spring at the top of this area so have shaped the creek bed to make the most of any water that flows, encouraging it to travel slowly and widen. That way, it will be a great habitat for native plants, frogs, and beneficial insects, and increase the amount of area that remains damp. Hopefully next time it rains, the deeper areas will fill and overflow out into the paddocks, rather than rushing away and scouring the topsoil with it," Squire finished.

Grace glanced at her father. She knew him well—his trademark rubbing of his chin with thumb and forefinger as being contemplative respect. "I'm impressed, Squire. You've thought this out well," Martin said.

Squire gave a small flick of his head and scuffed a boot in the dust. "I guess I've had a lot of years on Tullagulla to study the lay of the land and the nature of the soil, especially after rain. When I die, I'd like to leave the property in a better state than I found it."

Grace stood in quiet awe, drinking in the amount of work that had occurred and excitement blossomed in her. This was exactly the type of land improvement she and Tom had discussed with Squire—and now to see it unfolding was nothing short of exhilarating.

"Are you going to tell them the rest, Squire?" Lou asked.

Grace was intrigued, and her eyes met Squires'.

He grinned slowly and took Lou's hand. "Right where we're standing, is the site for our new home."

"Really?" Bronte clapped her hands together and beamed.

"Don't get too excited, love. It's not going to happen overnight. I'd like to build a small cottage here—nothing flash. Probably two bedrooms so the children can come and stay, with a wide veranda all the way around where we can sit and enjoy the view, regardless of the weather."

"What about your leather work?" Grace asked.

"We've got that sorted." He pointed to a Casuarina grove fifty metres away. "Over there, near those trees. It'll be a long, one-room building, again with a veranda along the front, facing the creek. I'll have one end and Lou can have the other for painting."

Lou flushed bright pink, and Grace studied her for a moment. In the few months since she'd arrived on Tullagulla, Lou had blossomed. Her grey hair appeared thicker, and its stylish cut was soft around her face. The strength and suppleness that her body had gained with hard work and obvious happiness defied her age. Grace wiggled her swelling toes in her boots and sighed. She was the one who was feeling older than her years now.

"Who's hungry?" Bronte asked. "My stomach's growling."

She dragged one of the eskies from the ute and carried it to the shade of a tree. Admiration amongst the group morphed into animated chatter while they ate their sandwiches. Beth and Margot remained under the tree with Grace when Squire led the others down to the creek bed for a more detailed inspection of the site. Lou was first to return, and she flopped, panting, into a folding chair.

"What are your children doing this Christmas, Lou?" Grace asked.

"Pip has a new boyfriend and has gone to Scotland with him for Christmas and Hogmanay."

"Hogmanay?" Margot asked.

"New year celebrations. It's a Scottish tradition that involves 'first-footing'."

Margot prompted her again. "More explanation please?"

"The ritual is for the first-footers to head for the homes of loved ones and become the first person to cross the threshold in the new year. Custom decrees that the first-footer sets the precedent for the incoming year and is welcomed with traditional Scottish hospitality—a wee dram of whisky."

"Oh," Margot exclaimed. "What a lovely tradition."

Her tone was unconvincing, and Lou grinned. "It is. Don't worry, Margot. I had heard of it but had to google the details myself."

"And what about Aaron?" Grace asked.

"He's staying in Cairns as they're doing some sort of study of the Barrier Reef. I'm not sure exactly, but apparently it has to be conducted while certain currents are prevalent, which is around Christmas."

The women sat in peaceful silence for a few moments.

"Isn't this the most beautiful place imaginable?" Lou

breathed softly. "I love that it has just enough height to be able to see right across the paddocks to those hills in the distance. And it is so peaceful."

A butcher bird sang loudly directly above them, and they laughed.

"Except for the wildlife of course."

Grace woke before daybreak and lay revelling in the quiet until the birds began their morning chorus. She tiptoed to the kitchen, a little surprised her father hadn't arrived before her. After a lifetime of being a dairy farmer, his days had continued to begin before dawn in spite of semi-retirement.

Grace drank a cool glass of water and picked up the milking bucket before partially filling it with hot water.

"Come on, Min. Let's get started."

The little dog trotted alongside her to the cow yard and flopped in the shade against the stables. Grace was greeted by Queenie's soft moo.

"Good morning, girl."

The calves bellowed indignantly. Having been sepa-rated from Queenie all night and denied access to her bulging udder, they were in no mood to be scratched and talked to.

"Hang on, little ones. I'll just get enough for the house and then you two can have all you like."

She scooped a dipper of grain from the container inside the stables and tipped it into the feed bin hanging from the front of the milking bail. After giving Queenie a gentle slap on the rump, she followed her into the pen. Then, squatting on the stool next to the big, black and white bovine, Grace washed the cow's udder with the warm bucket water and began milking. Queenie munched noisily, dribbling bits of grain on the ground for the overconfident and noisy apostle birds to snatch. Grace leaned her forehead against the cow's flank, while her hands worked tenderly, familiar with the rhythm of the *squeeze-stroke-pull* action from the years of practice helping her father. The bucket filled slowly with streams of pure, white milk until the cow's two front quarters of her udder were empty.

Grace stood and lifted the full bucket out of reach of Queenie's back legs before opening the gate and allowing her to greet her calves.

They bunted and sucked ferociously while Grace covered the bucket of milk with a muslin cloth and cleaned the yard. Min observed the morning's ritual with apparent interest, her head tilting from side to side as though hopeful for a small portion of the warm milk.

"Come on, girl. The others should be awake by now."

Heat haze already shimmered above the homestead and, with the exception of a myriad of bird and animal calls, the air was silent and still. No manmade sights or sounds disturbed the peace.

Lou and Squire arrived at the stables as Grace loaded the bucket of milk onto her little trolley. Squire led two of the older horses—Beau, the elderly bay gelding that Grace had enjoyed riding when Jarrah needed a spell, and Spike, the big grey horse that Bronte favoured.

"Morning, Grace," Lou called.

"Off for a ride?" Grace asked.

"Yes. We want to beat the heat and will shift those ewes and lambs into The Pinnacle paddock while we're out," Squire replied.

Grace waved and called, "The sheep will enjoy a fresh paddock but I'm not sure that you've beaten the heat." Grinning, she picked up the trolley handle and trundled the milk back to the homestead.

CHAPTER 9

In the house, the final day of the school year was facing a more frazzled start than usual.

"Come on, Maddy," Bronte called in firm, clipped tones. "We'll be late."

Margot was tying Daniel's shoelaces while he nibbled on a piece of vegemite toast and gazed into space.

"What's up?" Grace frowned as Bronte flew along the corridor towards the bedrooms.

"Maddy spilt her milk all over her costume." Daniel piped up.

Margot looked at her daughter and grimaced. "A bit of drama, but nothing we can't fix. Tom and your father have gone to help Greg shift machinery. If you take over here, I'll nip down to the woolshed and grab some more wool out of the crutching bin. We've got time to give it a wash and stick it on the costume before it's needed."

"Lucky she's a sheep in the play then."

Her mother shook her head gently. "Poor Bronte's a bit frantic. All that work she's put in. It probably would have been okay if it was winter. But she's worried that in this heat the costume will stink of sour milk by the time Maddy has to wear it and no one will sit next to her."

"Oh dear." Grace didn't know what to say. If it had been up to her, she would have let her wear the costume regardless of its smell. She shrugged and carried the bucket of milk into the cold room.

Within an hour, disaster had been averted. The milk-sodden piece of wool was removed from the costume, the supporting fabric washed and dried with the hair drier, and the new piece glued on.

Grace heaved a sigh of relief when Bronte and the children drove off in the Land Cruiser, laden with food and the precious costumes. Parents weren't expected to arrive until mid-morning, and Grace was grateful for a few minutes to shower and put her feet up.

The sun beat down as Tom, Grace and her parents trekked through the honeysuckle archway and opened the garage door.

Squire's ute halted metres away and he stepped out. "Lou and I are heading to the school now. Is there anything you want us to take?"

"No thanks, Squire. Bronte took what was important, and I think we've got anything they forgot." She studied his outfit admiringly. A smart blue checked shirt and moleskin trousers were finished with polished, elastic-sided boots and his 'good hat'—the Akubra he wore to town.

Hmm. Amazing how love and a family can change a person.

Grace and her mother slid into the back seat of her parents' vehicle while Tom and Martin took the front. Waving as they drove past, Greg and Beth's vehicle showered them with dust and Grace chuckled. Beth was wearing her favourite hat—a 1980s wide-brimmed straw version with a band of paper daisies around the crown. Every year when the paper daisies bloomed, she picked and dried enough to see her hat through another year or two, and, as it was worn infrequently, they did.

Parents and grandparents flowed through the gate, and greetings and laughter filled the air. They shook hands, kissed cheeks, and introduced themselves to the families with children enrolled to begin school the following year. In the end, the concert was a great success with the sheep and cattle behaving themselves and the baby in the manger not uttering a sound. The only hitch was when the donkey's head fell off— quickly rectified by the teacher.

"They're pretty good, aren't they?" Tom whispered to Grace.

She smiled at him, returning her gaze to the band of children as the music started. The audience were encouraged to join in as they sang Christmas carols. The principal explained they had a special welcome for a student attending the little school the following year. The boy was deaf, and the suggestion from a nine-year-old girl, who wanted him to feel especially welcome, resonated with them all.

Using sign language in addition to singing, they performed "Sing a Rainbow", concluding the concert. Grace glanced around and dabbed her eyes with a tissue. She was not alone in her display of emotion.

Lunch was a feast with, it appeared, many of the mothers competing for the unspoken 'dish of the year' prize. With opportunities to catch up with neighbours so few and far between, the adults moved around socialising while the children played and made the most of their final day.

Her head spun, and Grace fanned her face with a paper plate.

"You okay?" Lou slid onto the seat next to her and squeezed her hand.

"Yeah. Just a bit light-headed," Grace said.

"I'll get you some food. Don't move." She jumped up and walked towards the tables laid out under the school veranda. Light cloths were draped over the platters while battery-driven fly repellents spun furiously, dispersing any insects that dared to descend.

Grace picked at the plate of chicken and salad, flooding with relief as the dizziness eased.

"Better?" Lou asked.

"Yep. Much better." She smiled at her approaching mother and dragged a chair close for her.

"Daniel's been showing me through the school, and I've met some of the other children. It's lovely, and I'm so pleased we came." She smiled and plonked herself next to her daughter. Squeezing her hand, she asked, "Are you alright?"

"Yes, Mum, I'm fine—honestly. If I'm not, I'll tell you," Grace snapped.

"Of course you are. What time does everything finish here?"

Grace lowered her shoulders and plastered a smile on her face. "After lunch, most people hang around chatting until the kids are done. Tom and Squire will help pack up the desks and chairs with some of the other parents. But we'll leave when Daniel and Maddy are ready."

Margot nodded, distracted almost immediately by Daniel launching himself at her, laden with paintings, craft creations, and his school bag. He was closely followed by Maddy, still wearing her sheep mask. "Can we go home now?" she asked.

Grace grinned at Bronte, and she responded with a relieved smile. "Sure can, sweetheart. Let's collect your gear and take it to the car."

With the children leading the exodus, their faces smeared with melting chocolate Santas, it was another half-hour before everything was stowed in the vehicles and they said their final goodbye.

Grace flopped into the front seat of the Land

Cruiser. "Phew. I'm looking forward to that air conditioning."

Bronte switched on the ignition and turned the fan on full blast. "Enough?" She smiled at Grace, her fine, clear skin pink with heat. "It's so dry and hot—I'm sure I could fry eggs on this car."

Grace nodded and laid her head on the headrest. They waved to Martin and Margot as Bronte swung the vehicle around and pointed it in the direction of Tullagulla. Her appreciation of her parents, Tom, and Squire, quickly overrode her guilt over not staying to help pack up. She rested her hands on her bulging belly and closed her eyes.

For Grace and Bronte, the following days flew by. The list of jobs pinned to the fridge had a few crosses through it, but not as many as they had hoped. Lou returned to town to work a few more shifts at the hospital before her days off began, and the men were despatched to find a suitable cypress pine to install in the lounge to decorate.

The children danced around them, loud and over-active as they helped manoeuvre the tree into position. Then with Grace's help, they pulled the lid off the box of Christmas decorations and began dressing the tree.

Grace turned the television on while they worked, hopeful of hearing the latest weather forecast. She paused and stared at the screen as the map showed the progress of a slow-moving front that still hung over Western Australia. It had reached landfall and was causing destruction and devastation to many of the coastal towns.

"I don't wish damage on anyone, but it would be nice if we managed to get some of the rain," Grace said.

Tom looked up from his position on the floor where he was stabilising the bucket full of rocks anchoring the tree. "The experts are suggesting it might continue inland as a rain depression but doubt it will have any rain left in it by the time it gets to Alice Springs."

Grace shrugged and reached to drape tinsel over branches while Daniel and Maddy clambered around her feet, hanging up silver and red balls. "No harm in hoping I suppose."

As evening approached, the temperature rose, and as they sat around the kitchen table eating dinner, the lethargy in the room was palpable in spite of the air conditioning.

"We'll do the lawns in the morning, love, before it gets too hot," Martin closed his hand over Grace's, and she smiled at him. "You and I can potter in the garden while we let these ladies worry about the food depart-ment. It'll be like old times, won't it?"

It was true. Before moving to Tullagulla, she and her father had watched the sun rise every morning as they brought the cows in for milking. It had been her favourite time of day. The air was still and cool, and she adored the way the birds welcomed them with their vast range of voices and song. Her reverie was jolted to the present as Tom spoke.

"Squire's keen for us to shift the stock into the higher paddocks, in case we're lucky enough to get any of that rain over Christmas."

"I think Squire's being overcautious, but if it gives you both peace of mind, at least you won't have to worry. Lord knows how badly we need it," Grace said.

"We'll take the kids with us so you ladies can have free rein," Tom finished.

"Do you like the Christmas tree, Poppy?" Daniel asked, turning to Martin.

"I think you and Maddy have done a splendid job, young man." Martin smiled at his grandson.

"We're waiting for Cameron to come tomorrow night so he can put the star on the top," Daniel explained.

"Very good. It sounds as though we're going to have lots of jobs to keep us busy. You kids will need to help," Tom added.

Daniel nodded enthusiastically, and Tom ruffled the little boy's hair.

The men wandered back to the kitchen, with the children hanging onto Martin's hands and chattering non-stop.

"Where did you and Cameron meet, Bronte?" Margot asked.

"Cameron was working here with his father before he bought the surgery in town. They were painting Pepperina Cottage. Steve's a painter, you know, of houses and things. Not like Lou's type of painting," Bronte responded.

"I thought you knew that, Mum?" Grace looked at her mother and gave a small smile. She'd been reminded of her mother's occasional memory lapses during this latest visit—her father was often repeating things for Margot's sake. "I probably did. Just forgot." She continued blithely on. "What's happened with Henry's cat? Does Lou leave it at his house when she comes?"

"No. Pansy's getting old, so she brings her with her now. She bought her a special cat carrier with a bed inside it. Pansy loves it."

"She doesn't lock her in a cage, does she?" Margot looked horrified.

"No, Mum," Grace replied patiently. "She doesn't need to. Pansy comes and goes as she feels like it but never goes very far. Squire said when she's in the quarters, she does a little exploring, then either suns herself on the veranda or sleeps in her bed."

Margot dropped her shoulders, apparently relieved, while Grace continued.

"You should see Henry's house—whoops—Primrose Cottage now, Mum. Lou's planted the front garden with heaps of evening primrose to match the name plate by the front door."

Grace and her mother exchanged a smile as Bronte announced, "I'm making a cuppa, ladies. Are you joining me?"

Margot pulled out a chair and slumped into it. "Have you ever known either of us to say no?"

Bronte grinned and reached for the mugs.

Darkness fell quickly, and while Tom and Martin cleared the dishes, Bronte took the children by the hand and ushered them towards the bathroom.

They ran ahead of her before returning a few minutes later, freshly showered and in their pyjamas. Bronte's hair was dishevelled and the front of her shirt soaking wet. "Amazing how much water can still get splashed around when you're dealing with kids. They don't seem to care how far afield a two-minute shower can spread." She laughed and rubbed a towel over her face and neck.

"Mum, it's your turn to read a story," Daniel said.

Grace smiled at her son. "How about Nanny reads to you tonight?"

"Yes. I think it's my turn. Come on, both of you. Let's go and see what books we can find." Margot took each child by the hand and they left the room.

"You look as though you're ready for bed too, love," Tom said, and Grace turned her face to him. He was such a kind, loving man, and her heart melted. Following the tumultuous years with Pete, Grace's second husband continued to surprise her with his understanding and sensitivity. He was intelligent, respectful, and he adored both her and Daniel as much as they did him.

A child doesn't have to be born to someone for them to be a wonderful parent.

"I am a bit." She pushed her chair back and rose.

"You go. I'll be in shortly."

Tom's gaze warmed her back as she gave her father a quick hug and walked down the corridor.

After stopping at the children's bedroom, she tucked them in, then trailed into the en suite and stripped off her clothes. She turned on the shower and stepped under it, letting the cool water run down her back. Washing hastily, conscious of the dwindling supply of rainwater, she closed her eyes as the spray ran over her face. Three more weeks. Then the baby would arrive. Perhaps she had been too ambitious thinking she could host three functions in a row. She dried herself off and lay on the bed.

No. It's just the heat.

Fingers of light played on the bedroom wall, stirring Grace's consciousness. She glanced at the clock—4:45– and snuggled against Tom's back. His breathing was deep and regular, and she inhaled the scent of her husband's soap and aftershave. Then she slipped quietly out of bed.

Dressing in shorts and a baggy shirt, she cast a look at the lump in the bed and tiptoed out of the room.

Martin was sitting at the kitchen table, a steaming mug of tea in his hand.

"I should have known I wouldn't beat you out of bed a second time," she said.

"I'll pour your tea," he replied, grinning.

Taking their drinks with them, they crept stealthily outside and pulled on boots. The air promised a hint of moisture, and already the temperature was in the high twenties.

"If I was at home, I'd reckon we're in for a storm this afternoon," Martin said.

"Maybe on the coast you would, but I doubt it'll happen out here," Grace answered, looking up at the haze.

Min and Willow sat at Grace's feet while she and her father studied the sky.

"Come on, Dad. Let's get some weeding and the garden edges done—then you can whizz around on the ride-on mower after breakfast. Is that okay?"

Martin gave a weak salute and grinned. "Yes, ma'am."

For the next hour, they pottered in the homestead garden, accompanied by birds song. The windmill creaked as it gave an occasional turn in the early morning breeze, and the cedar tree cast its shadow across the yard. While the pile of weeds in the wheelbarrow grew, the heat from the sun strengthened, and the iron roof of the house crackled and groaned.

The screen door banged, and Grace looked up and smiled as Tom walked towards them in his socked feet.

He paused and squinted at the sun as he polished his glasses. "You two were up early."

"Can't lie around all day like some people," Martin quipped.

"Bronte's cooking breakfast—in case you're interested." He readjusted the frames on his face.

"Super. I'm ready for a break anyway," Grace said. "My back's had enough."

Tom hauled Grace to her feet.

"The roses look gorgeous, don't they?" she said. "Did you notice Henry's rose, Dad? We planted that apricot one for him. It's called Honey Perfume and smells similar to a mixture of spices. I think he would have loved it."

"Yes, you wonder how they can look so good when it's so dry and hot. Lucky though—no doubt you will be picking them for the wedding?" Martin said.

"We certainly will. Bronte wants to carry some of the blooms from her mother's rose bush in her bouquet too, but I won't pick them until the morning of the wedding in case they wilt."

Martin nodded and turned back to Tom. "Need a hand shifting the stock, mate?"

"Sure. That would be great. Many hands make light work. What are your plans, Grace?"

"After breakfast, Dad's going to run the mower around the lawns for me, then he can help you if you like. Mum, Bronte, and I are preparing as much food as we can so we have as little to do as possible by Christmas Eve." She took a deep breath and wrinkled her forehead. "The kids want to ride the ponies today. I reckon it'll be too hot for them to muster on horseback. Do you agree?"

"Definitely." He shook his head. "We'll bring the cattle from the open plains paddock into the higher and more sheltered paddocks. Squire and Greg will use the bikes, and your dad and I can take the kids with us in the ute."

Grace nodded and followed Tom up the steps where they were greeted by the delicious smell of bacon and the high-pitched voices of children.

The rumble of the old ute and the slamming of a door announced their return. The sun beat down relentlessly, and Grace grinned at the dust-coated children as they ran towards the house.

She opened the screen and passed a clean towel to Tom. "Laundry for you lot," she ordered.

The children followed Tom into the room at the foot of the steps, and climbed onto the box in front of the old concrete tub. It was habit for everyone to scrub hands and face and remove any heavily soiled clothing in the laundry before coming inside.

"We got all the cattle shifted, Mum," Daniel said. "Except the bulls."

"Oh." She looked at Tom. "What are you doing with them?"

"They're okay where they are in the scrub paddock. They're well away from low-lying ground, so we'll leave them in peace. Squire's bringing the last of the ewes and lambs up to The Pinnacle paddock this afternoon, and we've opened gates so the wethers can spread themselves out. The kids and I'll go back out this afternoon and bring them closer when we check the bores and water troughs," Tom finished.

Grace looked longingly at the sky. "Do you really think we'll get rain?"

Tom shrugged. "Don't get your hopes up. The weather patterns seem to be unpredictable. Even the meteorologists can't figure them out. If we get the animals sorted today and tomorrow, we can enjoy our days off and not have to worry."

Grace nodded in agreement. In addition to establishing regenerative pasture and drought-resistant feed, they had put so much work into improving genetics in their stock. The last thing she wanted was to have a repeat of the devastation they'd endured during her first year on Tullagulla. Memories of working with Squire dragging dead sheep out of the tangled barbed wire still haunted her.

Margot placed bowls of potato and green salads on the table, while Bronte sliced cold meat. Grace helped herself, mentally ticking off her to-do list as she ate. She had cleaned the bathrooms and got to the bottom of the dirty laundry pile. Next was to finish wrapping presents—something she needed to do while the children were nowhere to be seen.

She looked across the table at the two of them and smiled. In spite of their dishevelled appearance, they were both beautiful little rascals, and Grace adored them. Her stomach clenched as she remembered the day they had gone missing, and her gaze rested on Min, asleep on her bed in the corner. Min's defence of the children facing the terror of a wild dog attack had cost her a back leg. But even with three remaining limbs, her stoic and devoted obedience knew no boundaries. She could still jump up behind Grace in the saddle, muster a mob of sheep without pausing, and fitted in with any other animal or person she had cause to meet. Now ten years old, Grace hoped and prayed the little dog would still be here for many more years yet.

"Okay, ladies. Here's what we still have to make," Bronte said, interrupting Grace's thoughts.

"I'm all ears," Margot said.

Grace waited, and Bronte grinned at them both. "I'll make a chocolate log and a cheesecake. Margot, would you mind beating the pavlova mix and getting that into the oven? Grace, are you happy to chop up fruit for the fruit salad please?"

Both nodded at the young woman. Once again, Grace was in awe of her friend's organisational skills and calm capability. It was only days until her wedding, and here she was concocting three days of menus for more than twenty people and cooking up a storm in the homestead kitchen.

When she had first met Bronte and Maddy, sitting in the dust in forty-degree heat, she had wondered if she had done the right thing in inviting them to Tullag-ulla—would a young, solo mother straight from York-shire ever fit in out here? A shadow of a smile flittered across Grace's face. Not only had Bronte fitted in, it was as if she had never lived anywhere else. The bond between Grace and Bronte was as strong as a good sister relationship, and as for Maddy and Daniel, well, anyone who didn't know them might mistake them for twins, even if rather argumentative siblings.

The afternoon disappeared too quickly for Grace. With the bedroom door closed, she wrapped presents for everyone before placing them under the Christmas tree. The pile had grown, with her parents' gifts now hiding the old tin bucket that held the trunk of the pine tree.

"Hello?" Beth called. She pushed open the kitchen door and beamed from ear to ear.

"Hi," Bronte said. "Welcome to the workshop."

Beth carried a large, covered roasting dish and whooshed straight through the kitchen and into the corridor as she spoke. "I'll put this in the cold room while you pour me a drink."

The kitchen was heating up as Bronte filled the jug with ice and rhubarb cordial.

Grace smiled and got out another glass. She would miss this delightful, caring woman. For more than thirty years, Beth had been the only woman to live on Tullagulla, and following her daughters departure to boarding school, Grace could only imagine how lonely life must have been for her. Since Grace's arrival on the property, Beth had been the best friend, guide, and confidante a young mother could have. Her eyes prickled, and for a fleeting moment, she was consumed by a wave of grief.

Beth returned as she had arrived, in a bubble of joy and excitement, and plonked herself on a kitchen chair. Bronte placed a glass of cordial in front of her.

"That's the pork I put in the cold room—just so you know. It's not sliced yet, and I've made the apple sauce. I'll bring it over next trip," Beth said. "How are we going, Bronte? What's left for me to do?"

Bronte smiled at her. "Nothing. How's the packing going?"

"I've done all I can do for the moment. Kirstie should be here soon, and I've made her favourite dinner—lasagne."

Bronte laughed. "Great minds think alike. I've made a huge lasagne for everyone here too."

"We certainly won't be hungry for a few days," Margot chipped in. "I don't think I've seen this much food prepared since my boys lived at home and brought all their mates over with them."

Grace smiled and stood. She walked over to the bench and picked up the scrap bucket. "I'll go and feed the chooks and dogs. Dad and Tom should be back soon, and the kids will be excited. Christmas Eve is such a magical time of the year, isn't it?"

As the chooks clustered around her feet, Grace watched with love and interest. Always busy, they scratched and pecked the ground as they clucked and squawked amongst themselves. *Just like children.*

"Wait until tomorrow, girls. You'll have more scraps than you know what to do with." She turned and latched the henhouse gate. "Come on, Min."

The kelpie needed no encouragement. She gazed lovingly at her owner as she trotted at her side. Willow had been lying under the shade of the cedar tree and she got to her feet and hopped over to Grace.

Bending to rub the kangaroo's chest, Grace winced as a cramp almost paralysed her. She waited for it to ease and stroked her stomach. "Still a couple of weeks to go, little one. It's just Braxton Hicks getting us ready." She didn't remember having these in her previous pregnancy either. *Thank goodness for Lou.* Grace had been grateful to Lou for many things since her arrival in winter, one of which was her medical knowledge and calm reassurance. Grace rested her hands on her belly and smiled.

If I had to choose only one person to be with me when this baby enters this world, it would be Lou.

A small red car drove past the homestead as Grace sat on the step and took off her boots. The vehicle headed straight to Beth and Greg's cottage, halting before the door was flung open and a slightly taller version of Beth stepped out and threw her arms around her mother.

Kirstie. Grace had only met her once on their way home from Lord Howe Island. She and Tom had called in to the Brisbane hospital to visit Beth following her heart attack, and Kirstie had been sitting with her dad. Grace was looking forward to getting to know her better.

Children's shrieks met her as she opened the kitchen door—together with the blessed cool of the air conditioning.

"Mum! Come and look at the presents," Daniel said. His blue eyes were big and round, and his dark hair was damp with sweat.

Tom smiled at Grace, a pale line around his forehead marking the position of his hat band. While his thick, curly hair was also damp, his face below the band was floured with dust, and his glasses wore a fine, brown film, shadowing his eyes. "We've just walked in and you can guess what the kids noticed first."

Grace laughed. "I can imagine. It looks as though you'd all better hop through the shower before we let the kids near the presents."

"Yeah. I'm on my way. The paddocks still have a pretty good coverage and little or no dust, but the track is getting really bad. After Christmas, I'll run the grader over it and tidy it up."

Tom leaned over and gave Grace a gentle kiss before turning and scooping Daniel up under his arm.

"Come on, mate. Into the shower for you."

Darkness had closed in around the homestead. The thermometer on the veranda still read thirty-five, but the air in the kitchen was comfortable and surprisingly quiet.

The phone rang, and Bronte answered. As she returned, she huffed and slumped in a chair. "Cameron's been called out to a difficult foaling. He said not to wait for him because he doesn't know how long it will take."

Grace squeezed her arm. "That's a shame. He'll be as disappointed as you."

Bronte nodded. "Yeah. I know. He said to tell you his mum and dad will be coming out on Boxing Day if that's still okay? They're looking forward to having a couple of nights here."

"How do you and Debbie get along?" Grace asked, glancing sideways at her friend. She had only met Cameron's mother twice, and had been surprised at Debbie's over-efficient, almost abrupt manner.

Bronte was silent for a minute, and Grace narrowed her eyes.

"She's nice. It's-it's just she's really strong-willed and a bit of a control freak. She scares me a bit."

"Oh, Bronte, you don't scare easily." Grace smiled encouragingly. "And Steve's such an easy-going guy."

Bronte screwed up her nose. "I know. But I'm kind of happy that we're going to live out here and not in town."

"Oh." Grace bit her lip and began serving the meal.

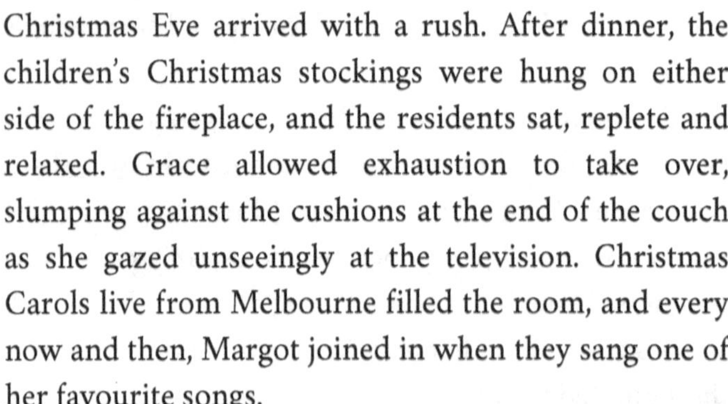

Christmas Eve arrived with a rush. After dinner, the children's Christmas stockings were hung on either side of the fireplace, and the residents sat, replete and relaxed. Grace allowed exhaustion to take over, slumping against the cushions at the end of the couch as she gazed unseeingly at the television. Christmas Carols live from Melbourne filled the room, and every now and then, Margot joined in when they sang one of her favourite songs.

Squire was having a quiet night at the quarters. He had reasoned that three days of celebrations and company were enough for any country man—he would wait for Lou to arrive in the morning and join in then. Beth, Greg, and Kirstie were also spending the evening together, so in the end it was only Tom and Grace, Bronte and the children, and Grace's parents in the homestead.

The lull before the storm.

The phone rang, and Tom strode along the hallway to answer it. Minutes later, he returned and Grace met his gaze.

"That was Tess. She's expecting Suzie to arrive before lunch tomorrow, and they'll be over about mid-afternoon."

"Great." Grace smiled at Tom and held out her hand.

He hauled her to her feet, and they returned to the kitchen to begin the ritual of making a final drink for the day as Cameron's vehicle pulled up outside the honeysuckle hedge.

Before she had time to call, Bronte flew past her with a wide smile. "He made it." Bronte's joy was infectious.

Grace poured the tea as Tom and her parents appeared in the kitchen. It was several minutes before Bronte and Cameron joined them, and Bronte's eyes sparkled in her flushed face. Tom reached out and relieved her of a laden box.

"That's the presents," Cameron whispered. "Are the kids still awake?"

"Probably—but they've been in bed a while now so are hopefully asleep." Grace said. She held up her crossed fingers. "They're excited, so I suspect it might be a short night for us all. Are you playing Santa, Cameron?"

Cameron laughed. "Christmas is so much more enjoyable with kids, isn't it?"

Bronte gave him a shove. "You're a big kid yourself."

"Yeah—that's probably the truth."

"Have you eaten?" Margot asked.

"If you mean, did I have any dinner—the answer is yes. I was just finishing when I got the call out. But if there's anything going for supper, I'm happy to oblige," Cameron answered.

Margot chuckled. "Cake, toasted sandwich, or fruit?"

"Oh definitely cake thanks." He shot her a huge smile.

She disappeared into the pantry and returned with a large, square container.

"Both Bronte and I made Christmas cakes this year, so seeing as I'm the matriarch here, you get to taste mine first."

Margot cut a wide slice of the rich fruitcake and laid it on a plate. Ruffling his hair with her other hand, she placed it in front of him.

"Looks awesome." He grinned and swept his gaze around the table. "Lucky Mum isn't here to compete with you both. Is no one else going to join me?"

Bronte met Grace's gaze and gave a wink.

Martin grinned and patted his stomach. "I'd love to, but even I have to admit that I couldn't fit it in tonight."

"Not for me either," Grace said. She rinsed her cup and bent over to put it in the dishwasher. "I'll check on the kids, and if they're asleep, we can fill their Santa sacks. Then I'm off to bed."

"I'll come with you, Grace—we'd better make sure we don't leave something out this year and have to answer awkward questions," Bronte said.

Grace glanced at the enquiring look on her mother's face. "Somehow last year we got their Lego packs mixed up. Not that it mattered as they were both thrilled anyway. I think Maddy was just puzzled as to why Daniel got the one she'd asked Santa for. We told her that Santa had been so busy, he got things muddled, and luckily Daniel was quite happy to swap."

Grace pushed the children's bedroom door ajar and

tiptoed to Daniel's bed. She bent over him and gave Bronte the thumbs up.

Within minutes, the Santa sacks were loaded, double-checked, and placed back on the hearth in front of the empty fireplace.

Grace yawned. "Goodnight, all. Coming, Tom?"

Tom followed her, turning back to the others as he went. "See you in the morning."

Grace closed the door and reached out to grasp Tom's hand. She placed it on her bulging stomach and stared through the window. The moonlight filtered through the flyscreen and onto the end of their bed. Outside, somewhere close by, a Boobook owl hooted.

"This time next year, we'll have another Santa sack to fill," she whispered.

Tom pulled her close. "I can't wait." He kissed her.

The baby kicked, surprising them both, and they laughed.

"We're nearly there, love. We've got the farm, each other, and will soon have another beautiful child joining us. Now all we want for Christmas, is rain," Tom finished.

Unease hung deep inside her as his anxiety matched her own. She kissed him back. "I know. One day soon, I'm sure it will rain again."

CHAPTER 11

Children's whispers and scuffling of paper penetrated the old tongue and groove timber walls of the homestead, blending with magpies warbling and the bleating of sheep.

Grace nudged Tom and leaned over him. "Merry Christmas," she said softly.

He mumbled and rolled onto his back. "Hmm. Merry Christmas. What time is it?"

"Almost five o'clock."

He groaned, rubbed his eyes, and promptly went back to sleep.

Grace struggled out of bed and pulled her cotton robe around her. She opened the door and her heart skipped with joy at the scene that greeted her. Daniel and Maddy sat on the old slate hearth, their Christmas stockings thrown aside, and the contents strewn over the floor.

"Look at this, Maddy." Daniel's voice rose as he ripped open a packet.

Grace flicked the switch, flooding the room with light and startling the children. They spun around, silent for a split second, and then scrambled to their feet.

"Mum, look!" Daniel squealed.

"Shh."

"Come and look at what Santa left for us," Maddy whispered loudly.

Grace grabbed a cushion from the couch and dropped it on the floor next to the children. She had barely lowered herself onto it when Bronte edged silently into the room, tying the belt of her robe as she walked.

"Merry Christmas," Grace said.

Bronte stretched and yawned. Slumping onto an armchair, she responded sleepily, "Merry Christmas."

Maddy threw herself at her mother, shoving a box containing a toy horse, rider, and accessories into her lap. "Help me open it please, Mum?"

Bronte grunted. "Let me get the scissors." She stood again and wandered towards the kitchen.

"Why don't you children go and wake Nanny and Poppy?" Grace suggested.

They needed no encouragement and ran at full speed down the corridor towards the caravan outside.

Within minutes, the room was filled with the sounds of Christmas—the tearing and scrunching of wrapping paper, Christmas carols playing quietly in the background, and the relaxed, easy chatter of Tullagulla's residents.

Tom and Cameron lolled on the couches, while Martin handed around mugs of tea and Margot ripped open a box of chocolates. "Christmas wouldn't be Christmas without kick-starting the day with a chocolate, would it?" She chuckled, and no one disagreed.

Much later, Martin was the first to move. "I'll go and milk Queenie."

"And I'll start cooking breakfast," Margot said. Grace began to get to her feet, and Margot held her hand up. "Stay there. I've got this. You and Bronte enjoy a lazy morning." She turned and hurried after her husband.

The roof crackled as the sun's rays beat on it, wakening the old corrugated iron from the cooler air of the night.

Grace stood, exhaling as she bent over and took Daniel's hand. "Time to get dressed, kids. It's Christmas Day."

A gust of wind whistled through the house, slamming doors and leaving a film of dust on every surface. Grace cursed and picked up the corners of the table-cloth. After taking it outside, she shook it firmly and returned to the dining table to begin again.

"Wow. Where did that come from?" Bronte pulled

the sideboard drawer open and gathered a handful of cutlery. "It's early in the day for a dust devil."

"Not sure, but I'm pleased I hadn't got around to setting the table," Grace answered.

"Lou's here," Bronte announced. "She dropped off a box of wine and some presents for the kids and has gone down to the quarters to see Dad."

Grace glanced at her friend. Bronte was speaking more quickly than usual—almost breathlessly. "And?" Grace said.

Bronte dropped her voice to a whisper. "You should see what she's giving Dad for Christmas." She paused and stepped closer to Grace. "The cutest little Border Collie pup you've ever seen."

A flush of excitement swept through Grace. "How absolutely perfect," she whispered back. "I can't wait to see it."

The children raced down the hallway and into the dining room.

"Can we open our presents from the adults now? Ple-ease?" Maddy said.

"Not yet. You know we have to wait until everyone is here—and that won't be until after lunch," Bronte answered firmly. "You've got your gifts from Santa, and you just have to be patient."

Maddy pouted and turned to Daniel, who stood quietly in the doorway.

"I don't like being patient," she muttered.

Grace caught Bronte's eye with the hint of a smile. She understood how Maddy felt—no doubt the reason why her own parents had waited until late on Christmas Eve to put their presents out when she was a child.

At midday, the residents of Tullagulla began gathering in the homestead dining room. Beth flapped around supervising Kirstie while assisting Bronte and Grace as they ferried salads and platters of meat into the dining room. Margot wrestled with the ice tray, tipping ice cubes into the punch bowl on the sideboard. Several missed the target and slid across the floor. The children scrambled for them and popped them into their mouths, oblivious of Margot's horror.

"Don't worry, Mum. They'll survive," Grace said, smiling at her mother's shocked expression. "I'll go and see what's holding the men up."

A car door slammed as Grace reached the kitchen. Her father, Greg, Tom, and Cameron stood on the veranda, drinking beer and discussing the weather —again.

"Come on, fellas. Lunch is ready."

The gate squeaked and Lou appeared, carrying a large, flat parcel wrapped in Christmas paper. Squire followed close behind, his attention focused on the contents of the cardboard box he carried.

"Merry Christmas, everyone," Lou called cheerily.

Tom leaned forward and opened the screen door.

"This looks interesting." He peered into the box as Squire reached the top step.

"Don't say anything. This little one is Lou's gift to me, and I want the children to get a surprise," Squire said.

Tom nodded and stepped aside as Lou and Squire edged their way past the men and into the kitchen.

Grace kissed Lou and Squire on the cheek and studied the small, black and white bundle curled up on a blanket in the box. "Isn't it adorable?" She looked at Lou. "Girl or boy?"

The lines around Squire's eyes deepened and his mouth softened. "She's a little girl, and I'm calling her Joy."

"That's perfect. I'm sure she'll bring you as much joy as Min brings me. You'd better go and show the kids."

She stuck her head through the veranda doorway and frowned at the men who hadn't moved.

"Come on, guys. You're holding up the works."

Daniel and Maddy ate quickly and slid off their chairs to study the puppy again. She woke and stretched, opening her mouth wide and showing a tiny pink tongue.

Anxiously hovering between the puppy and the increasing pile of gifts under the tree, the children breathed sighs of relief when the adults finished eating and cleared the table.

"We won't be long cleaning up, and then we can open the rest of the presents," Grace said.

Margot and Beth jumped to their feet and helped Tom and Kirstie scrape plates, stack the dishwasher, and hand wash whatever wouldn't fit. Grace and Bronte supervised the children's puppy play while Squire watched on, his bright blue eyes anxiously darting from one child to the other.

Grace glanced up before dropping her gaze again quickly. Lou held Squire's hand, and he leaned closer, appearing oblivious to the others in the room.

"How about we take Joy out on to the lawn?" Grace suggested to the children. "She probably wants to go to the toilet and she can meet Min and Willow."

Squire pushed himself to his feet. "We'll come too. Oh, whoops. Too late."

"She's done a wee on the floor," Maddy exclaimed, and Daniel giggled.

Squire swept her up in his arms and led the children outside, while Grace went to the laundry for a cloth.

Ten minutes later, everyone was back in the lounge, and the exchanging and unwrapping of gifts began.

"One at a time remember," Margot spoke sternly.

Maddy stared at her confused, and Grace elaborated. "Nanny means that we open the presents one at a time, so we can see what each person has been given and they can thank them. Okay?"

Maddy nodded and slumped to the floor with a sigh.

When Grace's turn came around, she reached for the large, flat parcel that rested against the wall. The tag read *Grace and Tom, with love from Lou*. She laid it on the floor and peeled off the paper. As the colours were revealed, Grace gazed at the vision Lou had painted. It was the Tullagulla homestead, standing proud in the colourful garden that Grace had created. The brick chimney reached for the white cumulus clouds against a blue sky, while the cedar tree filled one corner. Roses bloomed and, sitting at the foot of the steps, were Min and Willow.

A lump stuck in Grace's throat, and she couldn't swallow it. Her home. When she finally tore her gaze from the painting, she faced Lou and smiled. "Thank you," she choked.

Lou hugged her and whispered, "You're welcome."

As if Lou's picture hadn't been enough, Grace's emotions overflowed when she unwrapped her gift from Tom. Again, it was an original painting—a smaller one than the homestead—framed in tones of gold. Min's face peered straight into hers, and Grace's tears ran unchecked down her cheeks.

"I commissioned Lou to paint her," Tom said softly. "What do you think?"

Grace looked from Tom to Lou. "I think you have captured her more accurately than a photo could have. Even her expression is exactly the way she looks at me. Oh, Lou, you are so clever." She took the portrait in one hand and wrapped the other arm around Tom's neck. "Thank you. I love it."

"I have another little gift for you." He opened his hand.

Grace laid the portrait on the table before taking the package from his palm and unwrapping it. A dainty silver necklace, on which hung a tiny pair of stirrups, rested on the white tissue paper. "Oh it's absolutely beautiful." Her green eyes sparkled, and she turned her back to Tom as he held it up before fastening around her neck.

"It's handmade by a lady in Goondiwindi. Tess told me about her."

Grace fingered the stirrups and smiled. They tinkled, rather like a tiny bell, and the delicate chain lay cool against her neck. She reached up and kissed Tom before whispering in his ear, "You are the kindest and most thoughtful person I've ever met."

Over the next hour, Christmas paper revealed a variety of gifts suitable for everyone—handmade leather work from Squire: half-sized stock whips for the children and embossed leather belts for the adults, hand stitched and each with their initials stamped in the centre back. Books and clothes were distributed between them all. Each item had been chosen and given with love and thought.

Tom was delighted with the weather station Grace had bought him. Even without rain, Tom's passion for checking and understanding the weather had blossomed almost to obsession.

While the pleasure of sharing gifts and each other's company consumed those in the lounge, daylight faded.

Martin had nodded off to sleep in the corner armchair, and Beth, Lou, and Margot were deep in conversation at the other end of the room.

Grace hauled herself to her feet and announced, "Another drink anyone? Tea, cordial, water—or something stronger?"

The chorus of acceptances and variety of requests was enthusiastic, and Tom followed Grace into the kitchen.

"Gosh, it's getting dark already." She glanced at the clock and frowned. "It's only three o'clock." She flicked on the light switch.

Tom opened the door onto the veranda. "Holy shit. Come and look at this."

Grace stumbled to the back steps and sucked in a gasp. The sky was black, streaked with shades of dark green and violet, and the air still and silent. Not even a bird could be heard.

She and Tom stood mesmerised for a few seconds then stared at each other. Spontaneously, they hurried back to the lounge.

"Quick, everyone, come and look!" Tom said.

As the entire household poured out onto the veranda, Tom said quietly, "This is big. And it's close.

Squire, would you mind giving me a hand to secure the plane?"

Squire grabbed his boots. "I'll get ropes and chains. Be back shortly," he said and ran outside.

"Martin, can you and Bronte put the ponies, Queenie, and the calves in the stables please?" Tom continued.

"Of course," Martin nodded and grabbed Bronte by the arm. "Come on. We'll take our car."

"I left the windows open in the quarters," Lou said, her voice high with alarm. She darted down the steps, and Margot ran after her.

"Come with us," Martin called. "We'll check all the buildings."

"Greg, you'd better do a round of the generators and make sure they're fuelled up and ready to go," Tom called.

Greg grunted and hurried towards his ute.

They piled into the vehicles, leaving Cameron, Grace, Kirstie, and Beth with the children. Maddy stared at Grace then Cameron, her face pale and confused.

Before either of them had a chance to comment, Beth said, "It's alright, sweetie. We need to get ready for strong winds and a wild storm. It may go around us, but it's best we make sure there's nothing lying around that can blow away or cause damage. Cameron will stay with us while we tidy up." She paused. "Kirstie, run over to our house and shut all the doors and windows and put the rubbish bin in the garage." She turned and faced Cameron. "The trampoline?"

"We'll unhook the canopy and flip it over. Can you give me a hand, Grace?"

He hurried down the steps, followed by Grace and the children. Beth was slower, however, after thirty-six years of living in this erratic climate, she remained unconcerned and practical. She shifted the chairs from under the cedar tree and placed them next to the veranda.

Cameron's fingers were strong and deft, and within minutes, he and Grace had removed the canopy from the trampoline and turned the framework upside down. They grabbed a chair each and carried them up the steps, repeating the process until they were all stacked and roped together in a bundle against the wall.

"The flowers!" Grace yelled.

Cameron looked at her blankly.

"I've got to pick flowers for the wedding or they'll be ruined by the rain." She hurried to the garden locker and dragged out two buckets and a pair of secateurs. Working quickly, she half-filled the buckets with water before snipping as many roses as she could from the 'Rosemary' rose bush. After plunging their stems into the bucket, she continued until both buckets were packed with the delicately scented flowers.

"I'll carry them," Cameron said, snatching them from her and hurrying away.

"Put them in the laundry," she called.

Grace looked around her. Darting forward, she gathered the cushions from the veranda sofa and shoved them into the outdoor cabinet. She locked the door firmly and returned to the lawn as Min shivered and whined beside her.

"Daniel and Maddy, take Min inside to her bed in the kitchen. Stay with her because we know she doesn't like storms," she called.

Daniel clutched Min's collar and opened the French door. The little dog shot inside, quivering violently. Willow lifted her head and hopped over to Grace, scratching at Grace's legs with her front paws.

"Come on then. You can come inside too," Grace said.

She ran up the steps and the kangaroo leapt after her.

A rumble shook the house as Grace switched the kettle on.

"I'm frightened." Maddy wrapped her arm around Grace's leg.

"It's okay, love. You're safe. How about you and Daniel bring the puppy into the kitchen?"

Daniel's anxious face relaxed briefly, and he sped down the hallway towards the lounge.

"I'll help," Cameron said as the door crashed shut behind him. "I've shifted my car into the machinery shed. I guess the others will park their vehicles under cover when they return." He picked up a full thermos flask and screwed on the lid. "If the power goes off, at least we can have a cuppa." He chuckled.

The kettle clicked for the second time as the children entered the kitchen, each clutching opposing sides of the cardboard box. They had barely lowered it to the floor when there was a loud crack and the sky lit up. The light flickered and died.

Grace held the kettle in mid-air, waiting. "One, two, three … oh!"

Rolling thunder shook the house and Maddy screamed.

"It's okay, kids. Come and sit with me," Grace said. She handed the kettle to Beth, who entered the kitchen during the thunder.

Beth put it on the bench. "You can do that, Cameron. I've been around and closed the windows." She sat next to Grace and drew Maddy onto her lap.

Cameron filled the thermos flasks and walked out onto the veranda, while Grace and Beth huddled on the sofa, the children gathered against them. The rumbling stopped, and for a moment, there was deathly silence.

Then it started—knocking sounds like cricket balls hitting the roof. The raindrops began slowly, building gradually for a few seconds until reaching a crescendo as torrential rain thundered to the ground. Daniel put his hands over his ears.

The door flew open, and Martin, Margot, Bronte, and Lou tumbled inside, water dripping off their hair and their shirts wringing wet.

"Is everything alright?" Grace asked.

"Yes. We left the car in the machinery shed in case of hail. Then we ran, which is why we got caught."

Margot laughed and grabbed the towel from the door handle of the oven.

Beth held her hand up as Grace disentangled herself from the children. "Stay there. I'll get you dry towels."

"You'd better bring a pile, Beth," Margot replied. "The others will be here soon, and they'll be soaked as well."

While Beth hurried to the linen cupboard, the rain crashed on the corrugated iron overhead. It swept under the wide veranda and soaked the old timber floor, washing away all remnants of dust as it flowed.

Grace's stomach churned. "Where are the others?" she asked as Beth handed out towels. Grace studied her father's face.

"We saw Greg's ute disappearing into the hay shed, and Tom and Squire are sitting in the garage outside, probably waiting for the rain to ease enough to come in," Martin answered.

Grace relaxed a little and peered through the window, straining to see anything through the torrential sheet of rain. A shadow wrenched open the veranda door and Tom entered, standing on the doormat while a pool of water dripped onto the floor.

Margot threw him a towel.

"Merry Christmas, everyone. All we really wanted was rain—and we've got it!" Tom was jubilant. "I bet Squire's pleased he cleaned out all the gutters last week," he continued, grinning from ear to ear.

"Where is Squire?" Lou asked.

"He's gone to the quarters to get dry clothes for you both, and Greg's gone to check on Kirstie."

Grace gave a shiver. "Is it just me, or has the temperature dropped?"

"Not you, love. It is cooling off rapidly. We'd better light the wood stove if we want a hot dinner," Beth said.

"I'll do it," Cameron shouldered Tom out of the way and grinned. "You lot get changed, and we'll have a warm drink."

Tom gave his hair a final rub and took Grace's face between his hands. "Rain, sweetheart. We're going to be alright."

Grace smiled softly.

He's right. Nevertheless, her stomach lurched with a sense of foreboding.

$\mathcal{M}$inutes later, Greg, Kirstie, and Squire walked up the path as a lull appeared in the rain. An oilskin coat covered Squire from neck to mid-calf, while his Akubra sat low over his eyes, shedding the water as it fell. Greg held his coat over his head, and Kirstie wrestled with an umbrella, clutching the towel draped around her shoulders. Their laughter reached the sanctuary of the veranda before they did.

After stamping their gumboots, they returned them to the motley line up near the door, then flicked the water off coats before hanging them on the wooden pegs along the veranda wall.

Squire pulled a bundle from under his arm and handed it to Lou. "I brought you dry clothes. Didn't think you would have escaped that deluge."

Lou smiled and reached for the bag. In spite of her tousled hair and wet, clinging clothes, her cheeks were pink and her eyes glistened. She pointed outside. "And what's more, it's not over yet."

The crescendo began again, blocking the remnants of afternoon light and crashing onto the roof and against the windows.

Grace poured the boiling water over the teabags and spoons full of milo in the bottom of the mugs before fumbling in the darkened pantry for Christmas cake.

"If the power doesn't come back on in the next hour, I'll fire up the generator," Greg said as he reached for a mug.

"I wish I'd checked the weather radar earlier," Tom said. "No power means no internet or two way either. I wonder if the phone line is still working." He jumped to his feet and strode into the office.

Grace strained to hear over the noise.

"Yeah, that's great. See you soon."

Tom emerged again from the office, beaming.

"I got through to Orden Downs. Alan said they'll be leaving in a few minutes. They were about to drive over here when the rain began, and he's measured seventy millimetres already." Tom's astonishment was reflected in his raised eyebrows and wide grin. "As soon as it eases off a bit, I'll have a look at our rain gauge." He huddled in front of the wood stove and rubbed his hands together. "Let's see if we can crank this up a bit. It's incredible to think we've had to light the fire on Christmas Day!"

"You're not wrong," Greg drawled. "Only remember

one occasion in all the years I've been here—and that was a good 'un too."

Grace caught Squire's glance as he nodded silently and squinted at the windows.

The rain continued pounding the buildings, filling every undulation in the ground. It swirled, muddy and fierce as it flowed, collecting twigs, leaves, and debris as it made its way towards the drains and into the dams. Trees bent and swayed, their branches sodden and wild, snapping and crashing to the ground.

Tom turned on the camping lamp and sat it on the kitchen table.

Grace swallowed and forced herself to concentrate. "What can I do to help, Bronte?"

"Give your Mum a hand to peel and chop up the vegetables?" Bronte answered. She turned and lowered the Christmas pudding into a pot on the top of the wood stove, allowing it to bubble away, ensuring it warmed through to the rich, fruity centre.

Grace stared at the flames in the firebox and returned to the sweet potato she was peeling. She allowed memories to flood back of her first week on Tullagulla. This wood stove had become her friend, eventually, as she learned how to manage its moods and quirks. Now with a new kitchen and gas stove, they rarely used it, except on very cold days or in emergencies. Today had become one of those, and with the gas oven filled with meat and roasting potatoes, the wood stove was a blessing. She slid the second tray of vegetables into its belly and latched the door.

Outside, a vehicle drove in, and a minute later, damp air poured into the kitchen as the door flew open.

Alan, Tess, and Suzie had arrived, and the level of excitement escalated. That is, for everyone except Grace. Her feeling of foreboding continued as the baby lay heavy and low inside her belly.

"How's our little mother getting on?"

Grace was swept into a hug, her belly pressing into Tess's thighs as the woman towered over her. Her perfume floated around Grace's head and up her nostrils. She stepped back as the arms loosened around her and breathed.

"I'm doing well thanks, Tess." She hoped her doubts weren't showing, and babbled, "And thanks for coming, especially in this rain. Isn't it lovely?"

"Absolutely perfect. We couldn't wish for a better Christmas Day," Tess gushed.

Introductions were made to those who hadn't met before, and Beth led the women towards the lounge.

"Now come and sit with the girls and me so we can confirm the plans for the wedding," Tess ordered.

Grace meekly parked herself next to Tess on the couch. Suzie was ensconced in the semicircle of women, one hand clutching a glass of wine while the other waved about, assisting her conversation. Margot, Beth, and Kirstie appeared to be listening attentively, smiling and nodding, while Bronte leaned forward as though she wanted to speak, but couldn't get a word in. She glanced at Grace and rolled her eyes. Grace stifled a giggle.

Someone had lit candles, and they were clustered on the table and along the mantlepiece. Daniel and Maddy leaned on their elbows facing each other, mesmerised by the flickering light in the centrepiece and daring each other to touch the flames.

The men disappeared outside again, draped in oilskins, their heads hidden under Akubra's. They had been gone only minutes before a rumble was emitted from the cold room, and light filtered down the hallway from the kitchen.

"We have power!" Bronte exclaimed, and everyone clapped.

The generator ran for the next three hours. It's volume competed with the rhythm of the rain that continued to fall in a steady, even flow while the Christmas dinner was consumed with gusto, music was played, and the drinks were passed around.

The sky was pitch black, lit only by the weak beam of torchlight as Tess, Alan, and Suzie climbed into the new Ram truck standing proudly outside the honeysuckle arch. After they had driven off, Grace slumped gratefully onto the kitchen sofa while her mother and Lou finished putting away the last of the clean dishes.

"There's no sign of this easing, but at least the thunder and lightning have passed and it's coming straight down now." Squire stood at the window, staring into the yard. "I think we might make a dash for it, Lou." Joy was squirming in his arms, her little pink tongue licking his beard. "It's too wet to even put this one out on the grass for a wee. She's likely to drown."

Lou chuckled and removed the tea towel from her shoulder. "She'll just have to use newspaper tonight. Come on then. We'll say goodnight to you all and see what tomorrow brings."

Grace lay on her side with Tom cocooned against her back. The baby was still, and her eyelids drooped, lulled by the steady trickle of water flowing through the downpipes and the humming rhythm on the roof. Her hand slid to her throat and closed around the little pair of stirrups. Her breathing slowed, and Tom's warmth comforted her as she drifted into a dreamless sleep.

Christmas was over for another year.

Throughout the night, the sky continued to relinquish her load and, on Boxing Day morning, the residents of Tullagulla stood on the veranda, staring at the ongoing deluge. A touch of anxiety darkened Grace's relief. Tom had already recorded over a hundred and fifty millimetres, and there was no sign of it letting up. With the generator running the essential appliances, the internet was still unavailable, and they had only car radios to listen to the weather updates.

The solemn voice reverberated through the sound system, reporting: *A slow-moving front is bringing welcome, soaking rain to the inland and is expected to continue for several hours before reaching the east coast.*

"Several hours? When did the 'several hours' begin?" Grace asked Tom.

"Will it stop soon?" Daniel asked.

"Not sure, mate. It doesn't usually last this long, so I guess it will. Just think how full the dams will be now," Tom said, ruffling Daniel's hair. "We'll be able to test out that remote-controlled boat of yours."

Daniel shot him a grin and turned to Grace. "Can we play in it, Mum?"

"I guess so." Grace smiled. Any other time she would have joined them, dancing in the rain. She chewed her lip and thought about it. *Probably not a good idea. Wouldn't be a good look if I slipped over.*

Maddy shot past her and followed Daniel down the steps. Both children wore only shorts and T-shirts and within seconds were soaked to the skin. They spun in circles, their arms spread wide, and tipped their heads back with mouths open. Ankle-deep water lay on the lawn, and out across the track, gravel and dust had been transformed into a lake.

They skipped and kicked the water, shrieking and laughing until the breeze cooled their wet skin and they dashed back inside, shivering and covered in goose bumps.

In spite of the desperate need for the precious commodity, even Tom appeared to be jittery. The deluge washed under the houses, into the sheds, and their inland sea filled with swathes of floating dry grass and bushes. Sheep huddled together on high ground, and the cattle and station horses stood hock-deep in the water, their heads bowed and their coats dark and wet.

A rumbling drew closer, and over the top of the honeysuckle hedge, the roof of a green tractor edged towards the gate and came to a halt.

From under the tangled vine, two people hurried towards the homestead veranda, their heads down, protected by wide-brimmed hats. Oilskin coats camouflaged the shapes, and Lou and Squire emerged from the wall of water.

Tom pushed the screen door open and grabbed Lou's arm as she hurried up the slippery steps. "Phew. I'm glad I don't have to drive back to town in this," she said as she removed her hat and shook her hair.

Squire followed her in and opened his coat to reveal little Joy. He put her on the floor and shed his wet clothing, then picked her up again and followed Grace and Lou into the kitchen.

"What's it like down at the quarters?" Tom asked.

"Wet," Squire said. His mouth was serious, but the lines around his eyes deepened with the hint of a smile.

Grace searched Tom's face before answering, "Wet as in flooding?"

"A little, but it hasn't reached the floorboards yet

and seems to be flowing away without a problem." He paused and looked up at the ceiling, as if expecting it to divulge information. "I only remember one other occasion where we had so much rain in such a short period. This time I can see that the ground cover we've worked hard to keep has done its job." He smiled. "While water is lying everywhere, it doesn't seem to have eroded the land as it did in years gone by."

"I hope so," Grace answered softly.

The gate crashed shut, and Kirstie led her mother noisily through the archway and scurried up the path. "We're here!" she announced.

Greg hobbled after them, his limp more pronounced than usual. They stood on the veranda and stripped off wet boots and coats.

Beth screwed up her face. "Not so sure about our celebratory barbecue. I reckon we might just have to be content with yesterday's leftovers," she chuckled.

"Lucky we have plenty," Bronte answered wryly.

"Hayley and Nick can't come. I'm disappointed, but when they rang at six o'clock this morning, I told them not to. The last thing we need is for our precious family to be washed off a bridge and drown," Beth finished.

Grace started at Beth's blunt words.

It's true. We need to be practical.

While they waited for Alan, Tess, and Suzie to arrive, Greg and Tom set up the old slide projector, and Kirstie and Beth arranged the boxes of slides in order.

Squire ventured outside again to refuel the generator, leaving Joy curled up on Lou's lap.

Grace poked her head into the children's room where Martin had spent most of the morning. He was attempting to teach them to play simple scrabble in between assembling a Lego empire. Daniel looked up, his forehead creased and his mouth serious.

Martin winked at her. "My mate here is doing a great job with his building career."

"Look, Mum." Daniel grasped a small remote connected with plastic-coated wire to the miniature brick construction and pressed the green button. The blades on the windmill turned slowly. About to congratulate him, Grace closed her mouth as Daniel increased the speed and the head became more like a fan than a windmill. A volley of coloured blocks flew across the room as the structure disintegrated, and Maddy scrambled after them, roaring with laughter.

"Whoops," Daniel said, and they all joined Maddy in fits of giggles.

CHAPTER 13

In the darkened lounge, Greg and Beth excitedly relived Tullagulla memories. As slide after slide clacked through the projector and was illuminated on the white wall, their exclamations became more raucous. Those watching joined in, expressing laughter, astonishment, and sorrow as a young, dark-haired man and his slim, round-faced bride battled with an ancient Ford tractor, a sea of merino sheep, and kilometres of timber fence posts.

As the family grew, a pram appeared next to the woolshed, then a small bicycle, while a battered old Land Rover was parked outside a historic timber and iron machinery shed.

Another tray of slides later, a younger man in a big hat sat on a chestnut horse.

Tess's voice boomed. "That's you, Squire. I remember when you first arrived. You introduced yourself as Joseph Gentry, and your accent was so posh, everyone thought your surname was very fitting. We decided then that you would be known as 'Squire'."

Grace caught the look Squire shared with Lou, and a warmth deep inside engulfed her.

While the picture show continued, the ache in Grace's back increased, and she squirmed. After easing herself out of the armchair, she crept silently to the bathroom and leaned over the handbasin. She splashed cold water on her face and breathed deeply. A warm sensation trickled down her legs, startling her, and she stared at the puddle forming on the lino floor. She looked up at the pale face reflected in the mirror and clapped her hand over her mouth.

Have the membranes ruptured? What do I do?

Laughter filtered through the timber door. She pulled a towel off the rail and threw it onto the wet floor.

Rain still flowed along the guttering outside the bathroom window and pattered gently on the window hood. It seemed to be easing, but a trip to town would be out of the question. Alan had spent ten minutes regaling how he'd had the Ram in low range four-wheel drive and had still fishtailed through the dips while water lapped the door sills. Her stomach cramped, and the sound of waves crashing seemed to echo through her ears.

A gentle knock on the door broke her train of thoughts.

"Grace, it's me. Bronte. Are you okay?"

"Come in," Grace squeaked.

Bronte took one look at her and closed the door quietly behind her. "Oh, Lord. Is it the baby?"

Grace stared at Bronte's eyes growing round and large.

"I don't know. I think it might be."

Bronte rushed forward and grabbed the remaining towels from the hooks and rails, folding them to make an absorbent cushion. Then she helped Grace lower her unwieldy body onto the floor until she sat with her back against the wall. "I'm going to get Lou. Are you okay for a minute?"

Grace nodded, swallowing as she attempted to quell her rising panic.

Bronte returned as quietly as she had left, with Lou at her heels. "It's okay, Grace. I'm here with you, and you're going to be fine. Let's just have a look at you and see what's happening."

Lou's calm reassurance eased Grace's tension, and her pulse slowed as she concentrated on Lou's instructions.

After examining Grace thoroughly, Lou sat back and smiled. "You're going to have a baby very soon."

"How soon?" Grace whispered. "Can Tom come in?"

"Of course. We'll get you organised here, and Bronte will go and get him. Would you like your Mum with you as well?"

"Umm, no. I don't think so. Just you and Tom." Grace held her breath as pain gripped her and all thoughts were banished from her mind.

Vaguely aware of Lou's conversation with Bronte,

Grace's concentration stalled while the pain took her to another dimension.

"Some of those old sheets and towels … and can you ask Cameron to see what he's got in the car? A clamp of some sort for the umbilical cord … and a sterilised dish would be super as well."

"Okay. Got it." Bronte slipped out the door as Grace was consumed by another contraction.

For the next few hours, the bathroom substituted for a labour ward. While supporting, monitoring, and encouraging her, Lou and Tom remained with Grace throughout the afternoon. She walked up and down the bathroom, sat on the edge of the bath, and leaned on her hands and knees.

In the lounge, the slide show had apparently reached its conclusion and as the rain reduced to a gentle pitter-patter, the house quietened and Lou poked her head out the door. "Everyone's evacuated by the look of things."

Tom stroked Grace's forehead and smiled at her. "We've got the house to ourselves, so you can yell if you want to."

Grace gave a wan smile and clenched her teeth as another wave of pain gripped her, sending perspiration down her face and into her eyes. She blinked and leaned on Tom until the contraction faded before venturing out to do a lap of the lounge.

"I want to push," she whimpered.

"Okay." Lou grasped her arm, and with Tom's help, they led her back into the bathroom.

As the rain stopped and the setting sun shone its last rays from a watery horizon, a baby girl made her entrance. Small, pink, and with a tuft of golden hair on her tiny head, she blinked several times and stared at her mother from deep blue eyes.

Lou laid the baby on Grace's chest as tears streamed silently down Grace's cheeks.

Tom was quiet, and Grace glanced up at him. The creases on his face had softened, barely visible. He removed his glasses and blinked away tears. Lifting Grace's hand, he laid it gently on the baby's back then bent to kiss her. "She's just perfect," he choked.

Grace struggled to move. She was so tired, Tom had to lean his ear against her face to hear her. "Isabelle Rose."

He smiled and his voice quivered. "Yes, Isabelle Rose." He collapsed on the floor against Grace, and they sat gazing at their daughter, totally oblivious of Lou's presence.

While Tom held Isabelle, now fed and bundled in a soft, cotton wrap, Lou helped Grace shower and dress. She encouraged her to lay on their bed and rest. However, in spite of her physical exhaustion, euphoria had overtaken Grace, and sleep was out of the question. She couldn't take her eyes off the tiny girl lying next to her, and kept her arm bent around the top of the baby's head with Isabelle's body tucked against her armpit.

"Are you ready for the onslaught?" Lou asked.

"Yes. Let them in."

Grace beamed as first Daniel and Margot, and then Martin, Bronte, and Maddy hesitantly entered the bedroom.

Grace patted the bed next to her. "Come on, mate. Hop up here and meet your new sister."

Daniel scrambled next to Grace, his eyes huge and full of wonder as he stared at the tiny face. "She's beautiful." He smiled and reached out to stroke her forehead. "Like a doll."

As if on cue, Isabelle turned her head and stared straight into Daniel's eyes.

He giggled. "She's looking at me. I think she wants me to cuddle her."

Tom supervised as Daniel lay next to the baby and put his arm gently around her.

Margot hovered anxiously. "Do you think he should be so close to her yet? She's very small."

"It's okay, Mum. He knows what gentle means." Grace beamed at her son. "Would you like to go and see if Beth wants to come and meet Isabelle?"

Daniel nodded, scrambled off the bed, and ran out of the room.

Beth entered and beamed at Grace. "Well, this is a farewell we won't forget in a hurry."

"I'm sorry we stole your thunder, Beth. I didn't plan it that way."

Beth reached out and gave Grace a gentle hug. "Of course you didn't. I couldn't be happier that this day has been marked by such a perfect gift."

"Gift. Oh, Tom. Did you give Beth and Greg their gift?"

At first, Tom looked startled. It took a couple of seconds before he gave her a guilty grin. "Sorry, everyone. We've been a bit distracted. Hang on. I'll send everyone in and be back in a jiffy."

A steady stream of Tullagulla residents traipsed into the bedroom, followed by Tess, Alan, and Suzie. Standing against the walls, they watched on as Tom presented Greg and Beth with a large, flat box bearing a remarkable similarity to the parcel that Lou had given Tom and Grace.

"Open it," Tom instructed.

They laid it on the bed and carefully prised the tape from the paper. Beth lifted out the painting and stared at it.

Lou had captured the cottage that she and Greg had lived in for the past thirty-six years. It highlighted Beth's front garden filled with colourful geraniums. The house was flanked by the corrugated iron tank, sitting proudly on its stand with climbing bougainvillaea encasing the framework. The desert ash that Beth had planted the year they arrived shadowed the corner of the house, and the old picket gate invited the viewer to follow the flagstone path. In the left-hand corner, adjacent to the fence, was a section of what appeared to be an ancient timber shed.

"It's beautiful," Beth said simply. She sniffed, her lip quivering as she held it up for all to see.

"Thank you all," Greg breathed. "Lou, how did you know it so well? It's even got the edge of the old machinery shed in it. I worked for so much of my life in that old shed."

Kirstie laughed.

"I've had the devil's own job going through all the photos, trying to find the right one. That's why I asked you both to bring those albums down last time you came. Hasn't Lou done a great job though?"

Martin clapped and everyone joined in, startling Isabelle who screwed up her face and cried.

Margot bustled the crowd out of the room, leaving only Tom, the children, and Martin behind. They waited until Isabelle settled and Grace looked at her father. "What's been happening while this little one kept us busy?"

"Oh, we've been out and about," he replied airily. "You'll be pleased to know that the animals are fine. Squire checked the horses, and I've milked Queenie and left her with the calves in the stables. They're dry and comfortable, so you needn't worry about them," Martin said.

"And the rain? How much is in the gauge? Do you think it's over now?"

"Another hundred and five mils. So, add that to yesterday's and you've had about half of your year's average rainfall in two days, according to Greg." He grinned. "Not sure if it's completely finished, but the power's back on so that's a good omen."

Relief washed over Grace and she slumped into the pillows.

They'd had a reprieve. While there was mud everywhere and possibly damaged fences to repair, the long-term benefits of the rain would be nothing short of a miracle.

A tap on the door disrupted her thoughts, and Bronte appeared, carrying the old-fashioned kitchen scales.

Lou was close behind. "We're going to see how much she weighs," she said with a grin. "Apparently that's extremely important to your Mum and Beth in particular."

Martin chuckled and moved towards the door. "Righto. I'll be back later."

Grace unwrapped the baby and passed her to Lou, who laid her on the warmed hand towel lining the ancient steel bowl and shuffled the circular weights along the bar.

"Just under six pounds. That's about two point seven kilos in my reckoning," Lou announced. She turned to Grace. "Not bad for three weeks early. In case you're wondering, I've noted the time of her arrival as well. As soon as the road is traversable, we'll get you both into the hospital so the doctor can see what a great job you've done."

"Thanks, Lou. Once again, you've been with us when we needed you most. I can't thank you enough."

"You did a great job, Grace—and look at you now. It's obvious you've been down this path before."

"Mum, Isabelle can come to the wedding tomorrow," Daniel exclaimed delightedly.

Grace started. She stared at Bronte.

"I'm so sorry, Bronte. The wedding—have I ruined your plans?"

Bronte laughed. "I think you had a good reason to forget a few things for a while." She pointed to Isabelle. "I assure you, Beth is on cloud nine and will be talking about her special farewell for years. We've been to the woolshed and given it another once-over while you were slogging away here delivering Isabelle."

"Are the flowers alright?"

"Yes. They're fine. Everything is great. All you need to worry about is having a rest and looking after that wee one. Tomorrow I need you to be at my side—even if you have to sit down." Bronte raised her eyebrows.

"You know I'll be there. We'll all be there." Grace smiled and snuggled the baby closer to her.

CHAPTER 14

*A*ll around Tullagulla, water reflected the morning sunshine. In the clean, pure air, birds sang and trees dripped as the excess moisture weighed down branches and ran off limbs before joining the puddles on the ground.

Grace woke surprisingly refreshed. Isabelle had stirred several times through the night, however she had fed and settled again quickly, and both Grace and Tom revelled in their new family intimacy.

"I'm still on a high," she said, and reached for the breakfast tray Tom was passing her. "Hopefully that will continue all day."

Tom smiled and closed the door as he left.

Bronte and Cameron's wedding.

Grace sat munching her toast, reflecting on the first time she and Bronte's had met. The coincidence of her driving past the broken down car that day had been sheer luck, and at the time, neither of them had had any idea what good friends they would become—or that Bronte would be such an important member of the Tullagulla team.

Grace glanced into the bassinet and her heart sang. Isabelle's eyelashes rested on her cheeks, while her tiny rosebud mouth made sucking motions as she slept.

Pushing the tray aside, Grace tiptoed to the en suite and showered. Dressing with the bathroom door open, she was barely able to tear her eyes from the baby. After scrabbling around in the bag of bits and pieces she and Bronte had purchased weeks before, Grace extracted the baby monitor. She ripped the packet open, plugged it in, and sat on the bed to read the instructions.

Minutes later, she emerged from the bedroom, leaving the door ajar, not quite trusting a gadget over her own ears. As she drew closer to the kitchen, a babble of voices reached her, and Tom leapt to take her arm and ushered her to a chair.

"I'm not sick, just a bit tired. If I'd given birth in many other countries in the world, I would probably be having to return to work today," she said and shrugged.

"I know. But it's going to be a big day, and I don't want anything to go wrong."

"Nothing is going to go wrong," she said firmly. "What's happening with Cameron's parents? Is there any way they can be here for the wedding?"

Tom frowned. "Everyone's trying. Lucky Steve is so well known in the district. He and Debbie are driving to the first creek crossing at their end, then the property owner will ferry them across in his dingy. After that, I understand he'll take them in the tractor to the second creek, and if they can't drive through the water, they'll do it by boat again. Poor Cameron is a bit anxious about them, but you know what it's like out here—all our neighbours will chip in and help as best they can. Debbie is determined to be at her only son's wedding, and I can't blame her."

Grace raised her eyebrows. "Sounds like it could be an adventure they won't forget in a hurry."

With the rising sun and still air came the humidity and the insects. Flies crawled over faces and into eyes while mosquitos swarmed in clouds above the warm puddles.

Grace sat beside the old wooden bench in the laundry, attempting to arrange flowers. "Ouch!" She pulled the rose thorn from her finger and ran her hand under the cold tap.

A pile of honeysuckle vine lay next to the roses, and she snipped off damaged leaves and spent flowers, assembling a bouquet for Bronte piece by piece.

"It's all you're doing today." Her mother had ordered, and Grace smiled to herself as she took her time with the creation, her gaze alternating between her baby in the carrier next to her and the floral arrangement.

Vehicles drove back and forth along the muddy track to the woolshed, slipping and sliding as they travelled, carrying chairs, decorations, and the residents of Tullagulla.

At ten o'clock, Alan's Ram pulled to a stop at the gate. Tess and Suzie bustled up the path, and Grace leaned out the door while she wound florist tape around a stem. "Morning, ladies."

Tess jumped and slapped a hand on her chest. "Oh, you gave me a fright. I thought you'd be inside with the baby," she gushed. Stepping inside the laundry, she peered into the carrier. "Look at our dear little girl. Fast asleep." She hugged Grace awkwardly as Grace raised her arms to avoid Tess becoming tangled in the foliage.

Grace smiled. "How was the road this morning?"

"Not as muddy as yesterday, thank goodness, but the water is still flowing well. Alan and Cameron have headed back to the creek crossing to see if they need help getting Cameron's parents across." She looked at the bouquet. "Hmm, you need more greenery in that. Pass me those secateurs, and I'll go and find some—and I'll use up whatever is left to decorate the woolshed."

Grace did as she was bid, and Tess whipped around and disappeared.

"Go inside, Suzie. I won't be long," Grace said as she stripped thorns from the rose stem.

Grace twirled the bouquet and studied it from every angle. "You look okay to me. Hopefully Bronte will like you." Then she picked up the carrier in one hand and the bouquet in the other and pushed the screen door open with her shoulder.

Isabelle screwed up her face and wailed as Daniel came out of the pantry holding a packet of noodles. "Can I have these please?"

"Didn't you eat any breakfast?"

"Yes, but that was ages ago."

Grace smiled at him. His legs had got thinner and longer recently, and both he and Maddy had complained of their shoes getting tight by the end of school. *Must be going through a growth spurt.*

A vehicle splashed to a halt at the gate, while Grace poured water onto the noodles. Isabelle cried again, and Grace sank onto the sofa, lifted her shirt, and began feeding her.

"How are things going here?" Bronte asked.

"Okay. Tess is finishing off the flowers. What's happening at the shed?"

"It's all sorted." Bronte beamed. "Looks great and will look even better with a few flowers. Now we just need to wait for Cameron's parents to arrive and get ourselves ready."

Her excitement was contagious, and Grace grinned at her. Her clear, English complexion glowed, and her grey eyes shone like a lake under a full moon.

"I'm going to do Bronte's hair for her," Suzie announced, and the two women disappeared towards the bedrooms.

It was almost two hours later before Alan and Cameron returned to Tullagulla, conveying a jubilant, if slightly dishevelled, Steve and Debbie.

"We made it!" Debbie exclaimed, raising her fist in the air. She wore shorts, a long-sleeved shirt, and gumboots.

Steve was in similar attire, and as he slid out of the back seat, he hauled a suitcase after him and beamed. "Even kept the fancy duds dry, so show us the way to the bathroom!"

The welcoming committee, consisting of Grace, Tom, and Suzie, cheered.

"Follow me," Tom said. "Grace's parents are helping the kids dress, and Suzie and Tess have dedicated their services entirely to Bronte."

Cameron grinned. "I'll leave you to it and shoot down to Squire's quarters. I'm sure he and Lou will have me ready and in the shed on time." He jumped in his vehicle and headed off, driving considerably more slowly than normal along the track that had been churned into a quagmire.

Grace chased the flies from her face and followed the others inside. Her new dress hung softly over her slight figure, and she held the skirt around her knees as she walked up the steps. A calm, almost dreamy aura consumed her. It seemed such a long time since the previous Tullagulla wedding—hers and Tom's. It had been dry and cool then, and she looked around her. Mud now replaced the dust that had preceded the rain, and flies buzzed and crawled on every surface possible, while the heat haze shimmered in the distance.

I'm glad we decided to eat in the homestead.

She slipped off her gumboots and walked barefoot down the corridor to their bedroom. Isabelle was still asleep, dressed in a long, white gown made of the softest fabric and smocked across the yoke. Grace had found it in the chest full of Henry's beloved wife's handmade items that he had gifted her as a wedding present. The gown had probably been made for his own daughter, and as she and Grace's baby girl shared the same name, somehow it seemed appropriate for Isabelle to wear it on this special occasion.

Tom hurried into the room and laid his arm over Grace's shoulders as she leaned over the bassinet. "I think we're nearly ready. Cameron's trusting me with his camera, so I'm going to make the most of it. He can delete any that are not good enough." He grinned and stood back. Holding the camera to his face, he clicked the shutter as Grace lifted Isabelle from her bed. After flipping the viewer open, he smiled and showed Grace the photo. He had successfully captured the ethereal scene—a mother and her baby against the backdrop of a dark timber wall.

Grace tucked Isabelle into the crook of her elbow and picked up her shoes. "Come on then. Let's get photos of everyone before the sweat starts to show." She gave Tom a shove and followed him into the lounge.

While Tom clicked madly, Steve and Debbie reappeared, showered, groomed, and dressed in their wedding attire. Tess tucked a rose in the pocket buttonhole of Steve's shirt before turning to Debbie and pinning a spray of honeysuckle and maidenhair fern on her dress.

"I'm not sure that it's the right colour for me, but as I had no say in the matter, I guess it will have to do." Debbie sniffed.

Grace raised her eyebrows and clamped her mouth shut.

Hmm. So that's what Bronte has been anxious about.

Bronte, Tom, Grace and Squire waited on the veranda while, carrying shoes and wearing gumboots, the others filled the vehicles. Margot proudly held Isabelle before sitting carefully in the back seat with the baby, and they drove slowly towards the woolshed.

In the homestead and under the cedar tree, Tom took more photos of Bronte and Squire before they too donned their gumboots, picked up their good shoes, and made their way to the Land Cruiser.

Bronte reached out and squeezed Grace's arm.

"We made it," she breathed. A glimpse of sorrow passed over her face, and Grace clasped her hand tightly.

"Your mum will be watching, Bronte, and she'll be so proud of the woman her daughter has become," Grace whispered.

Bronte's mouth quivered. She blinked hard and dropped her gaze to her bouquet. The bright copper-pink roses they had planted in memory of her mother mixed perfectly with the creamy honeysuckle. She drew a deep breath and met Grace's eyes. "I'm ready."

At the woolshed, they added their gumboots to the array already lined up at the top of the loading dock, and Grace bent and helped Bronte put her shoes on before slipping on her own.

She stood and faced her friend. "You look absolutely gorgeous."

A hesitant smile flitted across Bronte's face. She dropped her shoulders and exhaled slowly before turning to face her father.

Squire stood silently by the open doorway, his eyes glued on his daughter and his face soft. The crisp, white shirt, navy trousers, and striped tie accentuated his tanned face and deep blue eyes. Grace had rarely seen him look this polished. He glanced at his shiny boots and reached for Bronte's hand. Tucking it into the crook of his arm, he gave both Bronte and Grace a smile that warmed Grace from her head to her toes. Then he paused at the open door, and they walked into the woolshed.

The ceremony took only minutes, and Tom continued to take photos as his confidence visibly increased. With the official part over, he photographed the newlyweds and guests inside the woolshed and out, incorporating many poses and backdrops for discussion and reflection in the future.

Everyone exchanged their heels and polished RM's for gumboots while Cameron set up the camera to take automatic shots, eliminating no one. Determined that nothing would be forgotten about their special day, Cameron insisted they include the dogs and horses— and finally, mud-covered vehicles that had conveyed the guests from the homestead were lined up to flank the happy group.

Through it all, Isabelle slept. Grace's energy was waning, and she was relieved when they returned to the house for the wedding breakfast. While the meal was laid out on the dining room sideboard and the drinks poured, she rested for half an hour with the baby, determined to enjoy every minute of this special day.

Hours later, Bronte hugged Grace tightly as she said goodnight.

"I know we didn't expect rain—or a baby—but today has been the best day of my life, and I'm so grateful. Thank you, Grace, for everything."

Tears pricked Grace's eyes as a glow settled over her. "It was a great day—and it's only the beginning," she whispered.

CHAPTER 15

Grace and Squire stood at the edge of the airstrip as the Cessna taxied towards them. Maddy jumped up and down on the spot, shrieking and waving her arms, and Daniel rolled his eyes at his mother. "They've only been gone for a week."

"You forget, mate. You missed us just as much when Tom and I were away."

He shook his head in denial, and Grace shot Squire a grin.

It was mid-January, and the weather and airstrip had dried sufficiently for Tom to fly Grace, Lou, and Isabelle into town. Both Grace and Isabelle were given medical checks and declared strong and healthy. The following day, the Cessna had once again bounced down the airstrip, delivering Cameron and Bronte to Brisbane, where they hired a car and drove to the Sunshine Coast for a belated honeymoon.

Bronte stepped out of the plane first and ran towards them. She lifted Maddy into the air and spun her around before setting her back on the ground, then turned and hugged Daniel, Squire, and Grace.

"Looks like you had a good time," Squire said.

Bronte beamed at him, and his eyes crinkled. "The best."

Cameron and Tom strode across the paddock, dropping the two suitcases while they greeted the welcoming committee. Squire silently transferred the bags onto the back of the ute before everyone piled into the vehicles and made their way to the homestead.

"Welcome home," Beth screeched and wrapped Bronte in a bear hug. "Did you have a wonderful time?"

Bronte extracted herself from Beth's arms and smiled as she prattled on.

"We're having dinner together tonight, and then the day after tomorrow, the removal van is coming."

Bronte raised one eyebrow. "That's come around quickly."

Beth exhaled and her shoulders slumped for a brief moment. Then as quickly as her despondency had appeared, it vanished again. "I'm making dessert and it's not finished yet. I've packed all my dishes already so I've borrowed one from the homestead. Better get back to it." She waved and hurried away.

"Well, you guys had better go and settle into your temporary home," Grace said.

"Not before I have had a cuddle of Isabelle," Bronte said, reaching to take the baby from Grace.

Isabelle opened her deep blue eyes and stared at Bronte as though weighing up whether it was worth crying or not. Then she smiled and Bronte beamed at her. "We're home again, little one, and our relationship is going to be a good one." She reluctantly passed her to Grace while Maddy scrambled into the back seat.

"I'm coming too," she said defiantly.

Bronte grinned and slipped into the front while Cameron strapped Maddy into her booster seat.

"See you all soon. We won't be long," Bronte said, and the vehicle drove away.

Grace watched until it disappeared behind the woolshed. A peace settled over her. Bronte was home.

The road to town had been declared traversable again —almost four weeks since the rain had begun, and after tonight's communal dinner, the exodus from Tullagulla would start before predicted storms arrived. Tom wasn't the only one anxious to see their visitors home.

For Grace, preparing dinner with Beth's help was like old times—before she had met either Tom or Bronte. A lump crept into her throat as memories flooded back. She pulled the leg of lamb from the oven and grinned as the delicious aroma of garlic and rosemary drifted around the kitchen. It was a far cry from the first roast she had cooked in the old wood-fired stove. On that occasion, it had been as black as soot and inedible, even for the dogs.

Lou and Squire were first to arrive, bringing the rapidly growing puppy with them. While Daniel rolled a ball along the veranda for her to chase, Bronte, Cameron, and Maddy clattered in, and within minutes, the homestead was filled with conversation, laughter, and the fragrances of good food.

Grace let her eyes travel around the huge table, observing the assortment of personalities that made up the group of friends and loved ones. The gentle and quiet, the practical, the bossy and the feisty. She met Tom's gaze and smiled as the baby monitor flashed, and Isabelle's cry penetrated the conversation.

Soon after breakfast, the first to say goodbye to Tullagulla were Cameron's parents. Steve had settled in well and seemed reluctant to leave. He had helped shift stock, cleared debris from fences, and towed fallen branches into heaps to be used at a later date for firewood.

Debbie, on the other hand, had argued—albeit subtly—particularly with Margot. She'd demanded turns in carrying Isabelle, demonstrated how vegetables should be prepared, and removed and rehung the washing on the line following Margot's efforts. While Grace had returned to her daily duties, she and her mother shared eye-rolls, and she noticed Margot's evening glass of wine had increased from one to two, or on some occasions more.

On the morning of their departure, Steve and Debbie assured Grace and Tom they'd had a wonderful holiday and Steve would be back to repaint the inside of Beth and Greg's house. Grace crossed her fingers behind her back and silently prayed that Debbie would elect to stay in town.

Grace's parents drove out an hour later, and in spite of the wave of emptiness that washed over her, it was time. She was ready to begin her new family life with Tom, Daniel, and Isabelle.

As they waved, Beth and Greg crossed the track and stood beside her until the caravan disappeared beyond the plumbago hedge.

"It's us next," Beth announced. "The truck will be here tomorrow at six."

"That early?" Grace said in alarm.

"We'll be fine. Kirstie has got us sorted, and there's nothing left to do except clean the house after the men have gone."

"Don't worry about cleaning, Beth. You know we're going to be working in there. You just concentrate on getting yourselves safely into your new home." Grace forced a smile while her stomach did a flip.

"I'm disappointed to be missing Zac and Rachael's arrival," Beth added.

"Me too. I was hoping to give that young fella a few tips with the machinery," Greg added.

"I know. Mother Nature certainly has altered a few plans this year, but it'll be okay. Now that Debbie and Steve have gone, they can stay in the shearers' quarters until the makeover on your house is finished." She reached over and squeezed Beth's hand. "You'll have to come back for a holiday so you can see it—and them. And Greg, you'll be able to inspect Zac's work and put him on the right track if you're not happy."

Greg grinned. "Dunno about that. My mechanical knowledge is mostly out of date now—and I never did have any training. It's all been hit and miss, and I've learned the hard way."

Grace didn't know what to say. She stared while a lifetime of emotions seemed to exchange between Greg and Beth.

Greg slung his arm around Beth's shoulders. "Now our new life is about to begin, and I'll make bloody sure it's a good one."

They turned and wandered back to their house while the sense of loss burned deeply inside Grace.

The following morning, on Greg and Beth's final day on Tullagulla, Grace was woken by the hiss of airbrakes. Seconds later, the air echoed with beeping noises as the truck reversed into Greg and Beth's house yard.

Tom dressed quickly. "I'll give them a hand loading

then bring everyone here for breakfast. Will you be okay?"

"Of course. Bronte and Cameron are coming to help, and you know the old saying— 'many hands make light work'."

He grinned and closed the door behind him.

Isabelle was asleep again following a four o'clock feed, so Grace made the most of her time alone to shower, dress, and tidy the room.

Taking the monitor with her, she checked on Daniel before heading to the kitchen. Before beginning the morning ritual of cooking breakfast, she pulled the milk jug from the fridge and groaned. It was almost empty.

"Are you on air, Squire?"

The two way crackled and clicked as his voice responded. "Yep. What's up, Grace?"

"Any chance of you milking Queenie for me? We're almost out of milk."

"Will do." And the two way fell silent.

Grace continued preparing breakfast as first Daniel appeared, rubbing his eyes sleepily, then Bronte and Maddy drew up at the gate on the quad bike.

Bacon sizzled, the kettle bubbled, and the peaceful kitchen became a hive of activity. While Daniel and Maddy played in the room off the kitchen, Bronte whipped up pancakes and Grace sat on the sofa and fed Isabelle once again. She had barely finished when voices drew closer and the kitchen filled with hot, sweaty bodies. Everyone was crowded in—Greg, Beth and Kirstie, Squire, Lou, Cameron, Tom, the two furniture removalists, and of course, Tullagulla's children. Chairs scraped and extra stools were added as they shuffled around the kitchen table, squeezing together with elbows touching.

Breakfast was demolished, more tea made and drunk, and Beth, Kirstie, and the men returned to finish loading the truck. Finally, the diesel engine of the removal truck rumbled into life, changed gears, and drove away carrying a lifetime of possessions.

Beth began her rounds and, one by one, those remaining were wrapped in the comforting warmth of her arms, tickled by her wild, unruly hair, and squashed against her ample bosom. Tears trickled down not just Grace's cheeks, but Bronte's as well. Even Squire shuffled his boots and turned away, pretending to cough as he brushed a sleeve over his face.

There was barely a sound as Greg and Beth climbed into the Land Cruiser, still plastered with mud and loaded to the axels. They lowered the windows and waved as they pulled out and drove slowly away, closely followed by Kirstie's little red car. The vehicle paused at the far end of the homestead yard, and Greg tooted the horn, sounding two long blasts.

"Leaving berth," Squire announced.

"Pardon?" Cameron asked. The others also looked at Squire, puzzled.

"That's what two long blasts of a ship's horn means. Leaving berth. It's Greg's acknowledgement they're leaving. I pray they have a wonderful life in the next harbour, and that it's a safe one."

Tom nodded, while Grace whispered, "Hear, hear."

Late that afternoon, Squire and Lou rode the horses to Allanga to check the cattle, while Tom took the tractor to cut a paddock of Lucerne hay. Cameron had been called to assist with a difficult calving and had not yet returned.

"I'm going to start sugar soaping the walls in preparation for Steve to begin painting," Bronte announced.

"I think someone's keen to get settled into her new home," Grace replied.

Bronte stuck her tongue out at Grace. "Of course I am." They both laughed.

Grace wandered outside and sat under the cedar tree with Isabelle on her lap. While she kept an eye on Daniel and Maddy in the sandpit, she swatted flies and gazed around her. She held Isabelle more firmly and glanced up at the sky through the filtered shade above, then closed her eyes for a moment.

A whisper shook her reverie, and she stared at the garden. Leaves rustled. The breeze increased, buffeting rose petals across the lawn. She gazed at Jane's head-stone before turning towards the sound of the children's voices. A sense of harmony descended on her, and she smiled.

Two young families lived here, and it became utterly clear that Jane had been waiting for the right time—that time was now. Jane's spirit was at peace.

Tullagulla is in good hands.

ACKNOWLEDGMENTS

Once again, my heartfelt appreciation goes to my husband Roger, my family and close friends. Your love, support and patience has encouraged and inspired me and I am incredibly grateful for everything you do.

Special thanks go to Lauren and Anna at Creative-INK, for your editing prowess and professionalism. Patti Roberts (Paradox Book Covers), I cannot thank you enough for your beautiful covers and so much more.

And you, dear reader, thank you so much for joining me once again on Tullagulla. I hope you enjoy this final chapter of the lives and loves of those we have come to know.

Thank you all!

TULLAGULLA SERIES

The Cedar Tree

The English Oak

The Pepperina Grove

A Tullagulla Christmas

FANTAIL RIDGE SERIES

Peninsula Promises

The Lupin Fields

The Scent of Promise

FEATHERWOOD FALLS SERIES

A Stranger in Featherwood Falls

Secrets in Featherwood Falls

Sparks Fly in Featherwood Falls

Clouds over Featherwood Falls

Coming Home to Featherwood Falls

A Festive Featherwood Falls

OUTBACK SKYE

Letters in Blue

Dust on the Heather

The Crofter's Song

The Cedar Tree

(Tullagulla Book 1)

Would you accompany your husband to a run down, sun scorched sheep and cattle station in outback Queensland to save your marriage?

Grace Campbell agrees to do just that, buoyed by the belief that isolation and rural peace will repair her marriage and provide a good life for her growing family.

But, as the ramshackle old homestead, shaded by an ancient Cedar Tree, unravels its secrets, Grace is swept up in the harsh beauty of the outback and its colourful characters. As if adjusting to a new and isolated lifestyle isn't enough, the handsome new owner of Tullagulla shows up and Grace is thrown into turmoil.

Torn between the gentle stranger and her hot-headed husband, Grace is forced to confront her feelings and question her loyalties, while her love for Tullagulla further challenges her ability to make a life changing decision.

When tragedy strikes, will a century old ghost help her or destroy her?

The English Oak

(Tullagulla Book 2)

She had nothing left to lose. At least that's what she thought.

Bronte Miller and her young daughter Madeline leave England and the only home they had

ever known when they venture to Australia in search of a new life. A job as Governess on

Tullagulla Station in the Queensland outback seems like a good place to start, however the

heat, flies and long days of work bring unexpected challenges.

As Bronte and Madeline settle into life on Tullagulla, the property is threatened by an

unexpected rural crime wave and its residents band together to assist the stock squad.

Then, just as a new relationship develops between Bronte and the local vet, a shocking secret

is revealed and her life is once again turned upside down.

Will she find the happiness she so desperately wants? Or will the hardships all be for nothing?

The Pepperina Grove

(Tullagulla Book 3)

A milestone birthday. A job she no longer enjoys.

And a marriage in tatters.

When her world comes crashing around her, Louisa Crothers is torn between fighting for the life she knows—or choosing another path–one she had never considered.

A holiday cottage on a Queensland sheep and cattle property catches her eye and Louisa heads west, searching for the opportunity to relive childhood memories, renew her passion for painting and allow the peace and serenity of the country to guide her decisions.

While Louisa settles into farm life, disappointment and regrets fade as she becomes embroiled in the lives and loves of the Tullagulla residents. A chance meeting brings an invitation to help paint a mural on the local grain silos while an unexpected bond forms between Louisa and the solitary station hand with a Midas touch for horses.

As heart-rending events unravel, Louisa is forced to appreciate the land and those who work with it and she finds herself questioning the value of her return to the city and all it contains.

Will she find answers—and happiness? Or is it easier to cling to old habits and familiarity, leaving her rural memories nothing more than a dream?